ANT CLANCY

GAMES DETECTIVE

Ruth Morgan

First published in 2019
by Firefly Press
25 Gabalfa Road, Llandaff North, Cardiff, CF14 2JJ
www.fireflypress.co.uk

A CIP catalogue record of this book is available from the British Library.

ISBN 9781910080993
ebook ISBN 9781913102005

This book has been published with the support of the Welsh Books Council.

Cover illustration by Sernur Isik
Cover design by Isabella Ashford
Typeset by Elaine Sharples

Printed and bound by Pulsio Print

To Geth and Steff

PROLOGUE

HOW, WHAT, WHY?

How do you become a games detective? Why would you become a games detective? Most of all what IS a 'games detective'??? LOL

Ant was chatting online with one of his mates from school, who'd picked up an advertising card from the local games shop.

Ant typed back:

Mate, you know sometimes you're playing a videogame and it gets glitchy or laggy, or you can't get up to the next level and you don't know why? Just bring your game round to my sister's flat and I'll sort it, np

He couldn't tell him the real reason for setting up the agency. He couldn't give away his suspicions about a very famous games company, or the discovery he'd made in Jubilee Park. He couldn't explain that he and his mates were looking for clues, waiting for Kody Crunch of Crunch Hut Games to make his next move.

Why had Ant started the world's first ever Games Detective Agency? Because the world needed one.

1
KISMET COSMOS

Six months earlier

Tarn's arm muscles felt like they were going to snap. He stretched even further, ignoring the branch creaking beneath him. Below – more than three hundred deadly metres below – the sparkling Arkenbarc River thundered between huge jutting rocks. Ahead of him, just beyond his flexing fingers, the rubyate key glittered in the zephyrbird's beak.

Tarn pleaded with the bird, 'Just this once. Please?'

Didn't he deserve a break? Not only had he solved the puzzle path in record time, he'd also sacrificed two of his favourite nordeaters to find this shortcut. Seeing those little fellas explode in the yatcha traps had been heartbreaking. But if he could claim the rubyate key, it would cut out days, maybe weeks of travelling.

'Pradahl,' yelled Tarn. 'Quick, come and help!'

Tarn's dragon Pradahl came racing out of the bushes, with coalberry juice dripping down her chin. This was good. Coalberries were a magical item which could temporarily solidify her smoke, if she'd eaten enough of them. Tarn climbed down and pressed the shining scale in the middle of Pradahl's chest to bring up her inventory. The coalberry icon said '5', meaning Pradahl had eaten five berries, so the smoke would stay solid for five seconds. That should be just enough time. He moved Pradahl into position at the edge of the cliff.

Tarn and Pradahl had been adventuring together for so long, they could almost read one another's minds. She breathed out an arc of smoke which solidified into a bridge leading straight to the hovering zephyrbird. Tarn raced over it and grabbed hold of the key. But the pesky zephyrbird didn't let go and Tarn had to pull with all his might. Any minute now the smoke bridge would dissolve. He had to hurry…

'Is it what I think it is?'

The voice broke Ant's concentration and he let go of the key. His avatar, Tarn, stumbled sideways and tumbled off the bridge. Tarn plunged to his black-and-white death while the zephyrbird fluttered off into the clouds.

No. What? No!

Ant tried to keep a hold of his headset but it was wrenched off him. He blinked. He was back in reality, back in the overgrown Dell on a bright but chilly Saturday afternoon in January. Children were squealing in the adventure playground on the other side of the fence. Three figures stood over him.

'Give it here!' Ant yelled.

Brushing the hair out of his eyes, he recognised his attackers and stopped. Ant was trembling with anger, but he forced his arms to his sides. He took a few deep breaths to steady himself and looked their leader straight in the eye.

Griff Landsdowne held Ant's headset just out of reach, like a smirking version of the zephyrbird. He laughed and the other two, Lyle and Boom, joined in as if they'd been waiting for his permission. They stared at the headset.

'It is one, isn't it?' said Griff.

'Is one what?'

Ant had plenty of mates at school but Griff wasn't one of them. He wasn't scared of Griff, though. Just because Griff's family were super rich, he acted like some kind of superior being. He had all the latest stuff, every new game or pair of trainers or footie strip, the minute it came out. That impressed idiots like Lyle and Boom but not Ant. Over the years, he had learned to just answer back and Griff would give up his mouthy overlord bullying pretty quickly. But right then, Ant was worried that if he tried to snatch back his headset, it might get broken, and he'd never get another.

'*Kismet Cosmos*?' Boom sounded baffled.

Ant kept still, his expression neutral.

'I think my grandad told me about *Kismet Cosmos*,' Griff sneered. 'Or was it my great-grandad? Honestly, where did you dig it up? Nobody plays this anymore. I don't know anyone who's played it, like *ever*.'

'It's dead, man. No one's played it for thousands of years,' Lyle added pityingly, shaking his head.

Ant forced himself to smile as they passed the headset around.

'You've got the gloves too?' cried Griff, like some delighted antiques expert. 'Let's have a go if it's so good. See what I've been missing.' He held out his hand.

Ant removed the haptic gloves, passing them to Griff like he didn't care. He really wanted to grab his headset and run for home. Ant was a good runner. But if one of them did catch him and jump him, his kit could end up getting wrecked. Much as he hated it, this *was* the best way.

Griff pulled on the gloves and crushed the heavy headset over his blond hair, which stood up in little gel peaks like a crown. He stood waiting for something to happen, tapping his foot impatiently. His eyes were hidden behind the headset's visor but Ant could imagine their outraged expression. Who on earth would *dare* make Griff Landsdowne wait? Lyle and Boom sniggered, but when Griff turned towards them, they fell silent.

'Start,' ordered Griff. 'Start playing, come on! What's wrong with it?'

'Erm … hardly going to be voice-controlled, is it?' suggested Lyle. 'Technology *that* old?'

'Activate it, then!' Griff turned towards Ant, even though he couldn't see him, and flung up his arms in exasperation. He really did have the patience of a three-year-old. 'Come on, Ant. Do I have to stand here all day?'

'Millions of years ago, apes worked out how to use switches and humans were born,' Ant muttered, reaching behind the headset. Griff flinched.

While he pressed the on/off switch, Ant also turned a dial, sending the game into energy-saving, 'flat-map', greyscale mode. Within seconds, Griff was killing himself laughing.

'What can you see? What's it like?'

Lyle and Boom grabbed hold of Griff's shoulders and shook him, but he was laughing too much to speak. Eventually he managed to say, 'It's pants! It really is … pants!'

Despite this, Griff persevered. Ant could see how quickly he learned to move forwards and backwards by twitching his fingers. Then he began flicking his arms around stupidly, while guffawing his head off. Ant could imagine what he was doing.

The flat-map mode had bounced Griff back to the very first planet in the game, Mantros, where he could do little more than run through the 2D woods, fire arrows and chase baby hommerabbits back to their burrows. On Mantros, he couldn't access Pradahl the dragon, which was what Ant had wanted. In flat-map mode, Griff couldn't harm the game or set back Ant's progress. That was more important than their teasing. They'd tease him whatever.

Lyle and Boom insisted on having a try and Ant had to put up with ten minutes of the three of them passing the game around and making fun. He sucked it all up. He had to.

'Finished then?' Ant held out his hand, as Griff finally removed the headset for the last time. 'By the way, you messed up your lovely hair.'

Griff frowned and shoved his hair back into place. He handed back the headset and gloves with his nose wrinkled and his little finger sticking out as though he couldn't bear to touch them any longer. 'This belongs in a museum, Ant. A museum of boredom. What's the point?'

'I like it.' Ant shrugged.

'But why?' Griff looked genuinely puzzled. Then he lit up. 'Soon as I turn twelve, I'm getting *Ray-Chay*. It comes out round about then. I literally cannot wait, guys.'

Lyle and Boom stared at Griff, awestruck. A 'Wow!' escaped Boom's lips.

Ray-Chay was the new game that everyone was talking about. *Race, Chase, Collect or Destroy* was its full name, but everyone was already just calling it *Ray-Chay*, including its creator Kody Crunch. It was the first game to give its players a full-body experience in a virtual world. Ant had seen the advert: Kody Crunch leaping out of his neon-green convertible sports car, flashing his million-dollar grin, pointing a pair of finger pistols at the camera and yelling: '*Ray-Chay's* going to change gaming forever. I mean FOREVER! Are you ready for the BIG ONE?' Crunch Hut made the best virtual reality games on the market, so everyone believed him.

Though long forgotten, *Kismet Cosmos* had been Crunch Hut's first-ever game, so Ant was sure that the new game would be absolutely brilliant. The main problem was the cost. The entire *Ray-Chay* set-up, including individually-moulded, featherweight headset and bodysuit, came to several thousand pounds.

'Get *Ray-Chay*, like me.' Griff grinned. Ant couldn't work out if he was being deliberately cruel or simply didn't realise that there was no way – no way on earth – he'd be playing *Ray-Chay*. It wasn't the age restriction: Ant had already turned twelve two months back. Just simply, Ant's family could never afford it.

'Maybe you'll let me have a go on yours,' Ant smiled back. 'Only fair, isn't it? You've had a go on my game.'

Griff's smile wavered at the idea that he'd let Ant try on his thousands-of-pounds suit for a split millisecond.

'The suit only responds to its owner,' Lyle chipped in. 'You wouldn't be able to use his suit, duh! You'll have to get one of your own, Clancy.'

'Didn't you know that? Keep up!' Boom made an ugly face, flicking his fingers dismissively.

Griff threw his arms around his mates' shoulders, pulling them towards him. 'Sorry, Ant.' He didn't sound it. 'See you around and enjoy your ... gaming.'

The three of them bounced away up the path joining the Dell to the Parade, laughing as though Griff were the funniest comedian on earth.

Ant watched them leave, overwhelmed with relief, cradling his precious headset in his arms. He was glad Griff hadn't seen the real *Kismet Cosmos*. It was too beautiful for him. So what if no one else had played it in years? Ant was one of the last, perhaps even *the* last, to travel from planet to planet in *Kismet*, in a quest to nurture the greatest dragon in the cosmos. That made it all the more special.

2
THE BIGGEST FUN

Griff's family owned the King's Elm Hotel-plus-Health-Spa just outside Westford Abbey, the biggest, poshest hotel for miles. On weekends, Griff would hang around the hotel, use the gym when no one was looking (you were meant to be fourteen to go on the machines) or kill time bothering the cleaners. He'd hijack their trolleys to ride down the corridors, build model towns out of soaps and packets of biscuits, and just be a general pest. Just be Griff, in other words.

After his twelfth birthday, all this changed. Not because he became more mature, but because of the *Ray-Chay* suit he received as his main present. He still spent a lot of time at the hotel, but on his own, in the main function suite, gaming. The cleaners were very relieved.

In late February there weren't many guests. One Sunday, Griff's mum was away on a theatre trip with friends, and his dad needed to catch up on paperwork. Griff didn't mind. As long as he could play *Ray-Chay* to his heart's content, that was just fine.

He changed quickly, peeling the suit on over his T-shirt and pants. It looked a lot like a superhero suit. They came in all colours and styles but he'd asked for a black one. It had small silver wings on the ankles and headset, and the red Crunch Hut logo – a small cabin being hit by a thunderbolt – emblazoned across the chest. The suit was packed with loads of tech but it was also incredibly lightweight. The bulkiest bit was beneath the logo, which was OK because Griff thought it made him look like he had a six-pack. It even had a red-lined cape.

The headset, with its weird-looking bug eyes, plugged into the neck of the suit with a short cable. It was skull-crushingly tight with hundreds of little suckers covering the inside, but you soon got used to it. With the full kit on, he voice-activated the game with just two words: 'Griff. Activate!'

His head felt fizzy, full of rushing clouds, as it always did at the start. As soon as this cleared, he did the three-minute calibration sequence to tune up the suit. A wise, old ghost-monkey character called Kyto appeared, sitting on a little cloud, and said in a calm, almost sleepy voice: '*Let me take you to another world, a world filled with beauty and happiness, a world that can be whatever you want it to be...*'

Griff zoned out, copying the monkey's slow movements, stretching his arms and legs, reaching from side to side, wiggling his butt in a figure of eight.

He was really, *really* hoping that today he would get to see his first enteo. He had almost completed the first three levels of *Ray-Chay*, which was training, all led by Kyto. Surely he was more than ready? Until you finished the training, you couldn't race, chase, collect or destroy the enteos. It was frustrating. Patience wasn't one of Griff's strengths.

Beginning *Ray-Chay* had been exciting and surprising. Secretly, Griff missed the adventure play centres he'd been taken to as a little kid: all the chutes and climbing nets and ball pits. He missed running around in the semi-darkness like a fool, chucking balls at his mates and collapsing breathless on the floor. The first time he'd activated his *Ray-Chay* suit, he'd been amazed to find himself in the best play centre he'd ever been to, full of big, 3D obstacles and tunnels which sucked you up and spat you out, until you learned how to control your movements. Slowly he got the hang of how to move. In the virtual world, you performed death-defying feats. In reality, all you were doing was making running, climbing and swinging movements on the spot.

The *Ray-Chay* suit meant you could sense everything. When Griff picked up a virtual ball, he could feel the weight of it in his hand. When he bounced on the virtual soft-play shapes, the sensation ran up his legs. The only difference was that in the virtual world, you never really got hurt. You could get whacked by some missile and it would feel like a puff of air, as though the blows were absorbed by the suit.

The main downside of the game was it could get kind of lonely. Griff had given his avatar a tough sounding name, YoBullit, but there was no one else in the amazing play centre to join in YoBullit's fun (Kyto the irritating ghost monkey definitely didn't count). Griff enjoyed being the only person he knew to own a *Ray-Chay* suit and he boasted about it all the time, but he sometimes wished Lyle or Boom were rich enough to afford one. Then they'd be able to play together. Even an enteo would have been some sort of company.

The enteos were ghostly, blobbish, constantly-moving creatures: dancing, wiggling and spinning on the spot. They wore large, shield-shaped masks in highly-decorated bronze, silver or gold. There were four basic enteo types and you could only be certain which type you'd found when it was unmasked. That was the game: when you saw one, you had to decide, was it a racer, a chaser, a collector or a destroyer? You had to study the stats floating around the enteo's head and look for clues in its movements. This took a lot of practice.

If you called out a racer correctly, you raced it. If you called out a chaser, you chased it. You added collector enteos to your cache. Then there were the destroyers.

These were the most difficult to identify. If you came across a destroyer enteo and guessed wrong it would 'destroy' you, which meant sending you back a level. Griff knew all this from Crunch Hut's website but he hadn't even sniffed an enteo yet.

He was swimming through sparkling bubbles down a red tunnel, like a single blood cell in an artery. Where the end of the tunnel divided, he shot down the left branch, out into a magnificent green chamber, like an emerald cathedral, containing the biggest ball pit in the universe far, far below. He stopped, levitating in the empty air. He was tempted to fall straight into the balls but he didn't. Instead Griff floated with total control. There: didn't that demonstrate his level of skill? He was more than ready to face his first enteo. So where was it? The suit must be broken. As soon as she got back from her weekend away, he'd get his mum to take it back to the store and complain, maybe win some compensation money for his emotional distress…

Griff stopped moaning. He almost stopped breathing.

There, levitating in front of him, so close he could almost touch it, was his *very first enteo.*

Griff had to act fast. The stats circling the shadowy shape's head were disappearing. They were strange codes and graphs but because Griff had never seen an enteo before, they didn't give much away. His heart sank. How could he tell what type it was?

The creature was cloaked in blue. The only clue was in the way it was moving, fiercely swaying from side to side — this was strangely familiar. Griff realised the enteo was making the same movements he had seen Kyto make in training sessions. Kyto would sway from side to side when he wanted him to chase light-filled bubbles around the tunnels. Had Griff found a chaser? It was time to take a chance.

'Chaser!' Griff shouted.

Slowly, slowly, the enteo removed its bronze mask. Its face was long and white, with half-moon eyebrows which made it look surprised. Lights from its eyes swooped around like laser beams and its mouth was a tiny, open 'O'. No matter what colour it was, every enteo of one type had the same face.

He was right! It was a chaser!

In a split second, the chaser had taken off. Griff followed it like the wind, out of the green cathedral and into a spiralling tunnel, down a massive helter-skelter, through labyrinths of different colours, up the sides of tower's and along high, vibrating ledges. He went as fast as he dared, remembering everything Kyto had taught him, completely forgiving the ghost monkey for being so annoying.

Every so often, he would glance nervously at the blood seeping from the thermometer. This meant his health was draining away. Griff was soon out of breath but determined to carry on. The clock was counting down, Griff could see it in the corner of his eye, the seconds ticking off one by one.

He was still a long way off when the chaser stopped at the end of a high ledge and looked back at him. Its tiny mouth smiled, its laser eye winked, and then it jumped. Griff watched it plummet, until it landed and dissolved into a shimmering puddle of fire on the crash mat, far below.

Griff had lost the chaser this time. It didn't matter. His heart was hammering in his chest and he was so elated he could have burst. This was the biggest fun in the world. This was the biggest fun he could ever remember having in his entire life. He just wanted it to go on and on. Forever.

3

A GIFT FROM LANCE

Lia was waiting in the hall when Ant got in from school, arms folded and, by the looks of it, ready for an argument.

'Why did you tell him?' she began in a quiet voice, which was never good.

'Tell who what?' Ant tossed down his heavy backpack. He had about three tons of homework to do that evening.

'Dad! Why did you tell him?'

'I don't know what you're talking about.' He'd had a brief conversation with their dad the night before, when he'd rung from somewhere in Belgium, but he couldn't remember saying anything Lia would have minded.

'Why did you tell him about Lance living here?' she cried. 'Anthony, you know it's only for a few weeks. You promised me you wouldn't say anything. You promised!'

Lia was Ant's twenty-two-year-old sister. She had moved in to look after her little brother while their dad, Snoz, was away, driving some duff old rock band round Europe. Her boyfriend Lance had also moved in, together with all his bodybuilding stuff. Lia and Lance had taken over the flat's only bedroom and Ant was sleeping on the sofa bed in the living room. This lack of privacy was why he'd started playing *Kismet Cosmos* in the Dell in the first place. The edge of the Dell next to the adventure playground had always felt like a safe place. Now he'd have to find somewhere else, because he didn't want his precious equipment being grabbed by those three mugs again. He still felt sore about it.

Lance was okay but he and Ant didn't have much in common. They hardly spoke, except to say, 'All right, mate?' and 'Pass the remote, dude.'

'I haven't said a word to Dad!'

Lia looked in his eyes and must have decided he was telling the truth.

'Then it's that flaming Hayley from number eight!' she cried. She dumped herself on the sofa. 'She's always either going in or coming out of her flat when I walk past. She's been spying on us, I know she has. She's always had a thing for Dad, she probably used this as a lame excuse to ring him.'

Ant sat down gently next to his sister. It was a bit of a family joke that Hayley from number eight fancied their Dad. 'Careful, Lia,' he said. 'You can't just run around accusing people. It might not have been her, you don't know for sure.'

'I wouldn't put it past her.' Lia began to cry. 'Oh, Ant. I knew Dad wouldn't like it 'cos there's not much room here. That's why I didn't tell him. But Lance has got this new job starting next week and we've nearly saved up the deposit for that flat in the Parade. Me and Lance living here was only for the time being.'

'I know, I know.' Ant patted her shoulder.

'It's been okay here, with Lance and everything? He's nice to you, isn't he? You get on with him?' She turned to face him. All her eye make-up had smudged so she looked like a pleading panda.

'Yeah, I like Lance. Course I do. We don't have much in common but he's a tidy bloke,' said Ant.

'Can you say that to Dad?' Her voice was going squeaky. 'Please? Next time you speak to him. Tell him you don't mind? Tell him we'll leave as soon as he gets back. I tried to explain but he just wouldn't listen.'

'Shush, course I'll tell him. It'll be fine.' Ant stroked his sister's hair and hoped he'd be able to talk their dad around.

'Hey, I'm sorry for having a go at you.' Lia tried to smile. She rubbed Ant's knee. 'It'll be great when we get that flat. It's lush. The kitchen window overlooks the Dell. There's loads of birds to spot, even a woodpecker, the old man who lives next door told me. You can come and stay whenever you want, Ant. We'll have so much fun together.'

'Thanks, Lia. I'll look forward to it.'

That evening, Ant rang Snoz.

'Sorry, son, I can't stay on for long. Death Spanners are due on stage in twenty minutes.' Death Spanners was the name of the band. As well as driving them around, Snoz helped set up the equipment and acted as security during each show, standing in front of the audience with his arms folded to prevent over-enthusiastic, sweaty fans from climbing up on stage.

'Lia is really upset,' said Ant. 'Honestly, Dad, Lance living here isn't a problem. It's only until you get back, anyway.'

'She should have told me. There isn't enough room in that flat to swing a cat.'

'I know, but Lance's landlord sold the house he and his mates were living in. He had nowhere else to go. You've met Lance. He's an all right bloke. You wouldn't want to see him homeless, would you?'

'I suppose I should be grateful his mates didn't move in too,' said Snoz. Ant heard someone in the background yelling his dad's name. Snoz yelled something back then came back to Ant. 'All right, he can stay as long as he behaves, but any trouble and I'll be catching a plane straight back, understand?'

'Understand.'

'Now, did you get your share of the money I transferred to Lia's account last Thursday?'

'Yes, Dad, thanks.'

'And you're doing your homework?'

'Course I am.'

'How's the table tennis?' Ant belonged to a local club and played regularly in competitions.

'Great. I'm through to the next round in the tournament.'

'That's fantastic, son, well done. How about your gaming? You got that under control?' Snoz sounded concerned.

'Sure. An hour in the evening on weekdays, two hours on Saturdays and Sundays. There's too much to do for school in the week, and on weekends, you know, I want to practise table tennis and meet up with my mates.'

When Ant had first got into *Kismet Cosmos,* he had become pretty addicted, playing every moment he could. One day, Snoz had sat him down and talked to him seriously about addiction and how it can ruin your life. They'd come up with the one-hour/two-hour rule and Ant was still sticking to it, *most* of the time.

'What do I always say?' asked Snoz.

Ant chipped in quickly, 'You've got to be bigger than the game.'

'Cor-rect,' said Snoz. 'Last question: are you eating properly?'

'Shepherd's pie this evening. I helped Lia peel the spuds.'

Snoz chuckled. 'Good lad. I'll text you tomorrow then, yeah? Send you a photo of the gig?'

Ant got a photo of every Death Spanners concert and they all looked the same: blue lights, dry ice and four leather-clad pensioners with long curly hair, posing with their guitars and drumsticks. In a way, it was quite cool to still be doing that at their age.

'Great, Dad. Don't worry about us, we're fine. See you in two weeks.'

'Love you, son. Tell your sister I love her too.'

Snoz ended the call. Ant knew his dad didn't like being away from home, but this was the only job he could get that paid decent money. They really needed it, especially since Snoz had volunteered to help Lia with her college costs. Lia's dream was to work with animals and she was studying to become a veterinary nurse. Even if money was tight, Ant reckoned he was lucky to have a family that always helped each other out.

When Ant told Lia what their dad had said, she hugged him and made loads more promises about the great times they were all going to have in the new flat.

Lance started making more of an effort too. His new job was working in the games shop in the Parade. Lance started talking to Ant about the kinds of videogames he'd been into when he was younger, some Ant had never heard of like *Speedster Valley* and *Blobber Dungeon.* For the first time, he and Ant were hanging out together properly and having really interesting conversations.

A few weeks into the job, Lance came home with a large carrier bag. He placed it on the table next to Ant, who was doing his maths homework. Lance had a massive smile on his face. 'Present for 'ya,' he said and stood waiting for Ant's reaction.

Ant pushed aside his books and delved into the bag. A suit unfolded into his lap. The headset stared at him with weird bug eyes.

'No. I mean no! Never!' Ant goggled at Lance.

'*Ray-Chay*,' said Lance. 'You must want it. All the kids are talking about it.'

'Wow, thanks!' Ant didn't know what to say. He was too polite to ask the obvious question: how on earth could Lance afford a *Ray-Chay* suit? Lance guessed what he was thinking.

'The shop's been sent these cheaper samples to try out before we start stocking them,' he explained. 'They're not made-to-measure like the expensive ones. Looks a lot cheaper, doesn't it? Not so superhero-y. It plays just as well, though, apparently. They sent us three, but this one didn't fit anyone: too small. I thought you'd appreciate it, so I asked my boss Daisy if I could bring it home for you. Going to try it on then?'

'You bet!' Ant said. 'Absolutely brilliant, Lance. Thanks a lot.'

Lia offered to keep Ant's fish fingers warm in the oven. Ant went into the bedroom while Lia and Lance settled down to eat their tea. The material was really stiff and Ant had to wriggle around to get comfortable. He looked at himself in the mirror.

The suit was a boring grey with a small, white Crunch Hut thunderbolt logo sewn on to the front with yellow thread. It seemed nothing like the amazing-sounding suit Griff kept boasting about at school. The stitching on the logo was coming loose and it clearly wasn't that well made. Still, if *Ray-Chay* was as incredible as everyone said, it wouldn't matter. Ant squeezed on the funny-looking, sucker-lined headset and plugged it into the suit via a short cable. Then he voice-activated the game with a code printed on a small tag hanging from the sleeve. Now the suit would recognise Ant's voice and only he would be able to use it. At first his head felt like a shaken bottle of pop, but the sensation didn't last long. A little old ghost monkey appeared, introduced himself as Kyto and began a speech, *'Let me take you to another world...'* Ant copied Kyto's slow, rhythmic movements for a few minutes before the proper game began.

It was weird. Ant found it impossible to focus on the shapes and colours, heights and depths. He tried to move and he fell over. He felt dizzy and a bit sick. Lance had warned him about this.

When Ant started making sense of what he could see, it was even weirder.

Surely he knew this place? Wasn't this planet Aneome in *Kismet Cosmos*? Ant walked a few steps and looked down. There, three hundred metres below, thundered the sparkling Arkenbarc River. Above him rose Warriot's Peak, majestic against the cloudless blue sky. When he looked down at himself, he was wearing his avatar Tarn's skin.

Ant really loved planet Aneome, it was probably his favourite planet so far in *Kismet*, even though he was now on a different level in the real game. Everything was right about this version, yet everything was wrong, too. There were none of the signs of life he was used to: no fluttersects, zephyrbirds or hommerabbits, let alone Pradahl, who was always somewhere nearby, usually getting into trouble. The ghost monkey was only there to give him training instructions and wasn't a real part of the game.

He knew it would take several *Ray-Chay* levels before the enteos began appearing. Then, presumably, the game would start getting as exciting as everyone said. It was impressive how much more he felt inside this virtual world because of the *Ray-Chay* suit. Yet what was the point, when Ant had a much more thrilling version of the game, where he'd already reached the ninety-sixth planet? There were still puzzle paths to solve and jewel keys to find in *Kismet Cosmos.* There were still new planets to fly to and fabulous dragon-skin suits to earn.

It didn't take long for Ant to feel bored. He deactivated the game and removed the headset. He wriggled out of the stiff suit, wondering if anyone else had spotted that this great new game was actually a shameless copy of *Kismet Cosmos*. Oh, but of course, no one had played *Kismet* in years, had they? Crunch Hut had simply decided to 'recycle' its first game, thinking that no one would notice. How lame was that?

Like everyone into gaming, Ant was a huge admirer of coding genius Kody Crunch. Kody and his twin sister Kelly had set up Crunch Hut while they were still teenagers. Kelly had dropped off the scene long ago and no one seemed to remember her any more. Kody had gone from strength to strength and was one of the richest, coolest and most successful guys in gaming, living on his own private Caribbean island. In each new advert he would ride up on a jet ski or land his helicopter on some spectacular cliff, point his finger pistols at the camera and tell everyone to buy his latest game. Ant thought the ads were horribly cheesy but the games themselves were fantastic. Up until this one.

Ant picked up his *Kismet* headset and ran his thumb over the worn Crunch Hut logo. 'How do you think you can get away with this, Kody?' he whispered. 'The game's so lame. The original's a million times better.' Ah well, it was disappointing, but even geniuses got it wrong sometimes.

That evening, Lance asked whether he liked *Ray-Chay* and Ant admitted he hadn't got into it yet. When Lance asked him again the following day, Ant said something similar. He didn't want to disappoint Lance but he didn't think he was ever going to get into *Ray-Chay*. He didn't see the point of it.

4
THE RAREIO

Four months later everyone was playing *Ray-Chay*. The cheaper suits had been released, which meant you didn't need to be rich in order to play. Griff was disgusted by the stiff grey suits, but he did enjoy the company. He'd promised his parents he'd only play online with friends he knew in real life. He knew never to get friendly with strangers online or agree to meet up, because they might not be who they claimed.

Every day after school, Griff would meet Lyle and Boom in his virtual adventure-play world, where they would race, chase, collect and destroy enteos together as a team. None of them realised that the worlds they played in were all different: Lyle's world was a war zone, while Boom's was a kind of monster-truck superdrome. The enteos they found were all alike, however.

Something else disgusted Griff: his mum, Paula, had bought an expensive, spangly, pink *Ray-Chay* suit of her own, complete with bunny ears and a tail. *Ray-Chay* had become popular with adults because it was a great, fun way of exercising. Griff made his mum promise never to leave the house in her embarrassing suit. She played in the huge master bedroom of their house because she feared crashing into real-life objects.

Paula loved romantic historical novels. Her favourite was *Heart of a Highwayman* by Crystal McNabbs. When she played *Ray-Chay*, she always found herself in a forest at night, her arms wrapped round the handsome, masked highwayman Will Carey, galloping along on his black stallion. Sometimes they climbed trees or abseiled down canyons in pursuit of enteos, daredevil feats that would have terrified her in real life. Sometimes, if there was time, they might stop for a little kiss.

Every morning, once Griff's dad Evan had left for work and Griff for school, Paula enjoyed her precious *Ray-Chay* time. Before long, she was very good. She could tell a racer from a chaser in a heartbeat. She defeated peak-strength destroyers with ease. Although it felt a tiny bit like cheating, she had found some great spawn locations, which meant she was really pushing up through the levels. Will Carey always stood by and watched her deal with the fearsome enteos, muttering encouragement in his deep, manly voice. It annoyed her that she made the decisions while he just stood there, but that was the game.

This time, she and Will were walking hand in hand beside a moonlit lake. Will's dark eyes glimmered behind his highwayman's mask. Over his shoulder, Paula noticed a peppermint-green, wispy shape floating at the water's edge. It was twice as big as any of the enteos she'd seen before. The stats around it made a kind of sense to her and she felt a pang of excitement.

'It's a collector,' she whispered. 'A rareio. I can't believe it!'

'Retrieve it, my dear,' Will muttered in his eighteenth-century way.

Paula took a few steps forward. The rareio raised its head and pulsed with an inner light, its golden mask giving nothing away.

'Collector!' Paula's voice rang out determinedly. She folded one hand inside the other, like a double fist, and placed them over her heart.

The rareio pulled back a little, resisting. Paula called it out again and again, feeling herself growing in strength. Finally, reluctantly, the enteo removed its mask to reveal its telltale collector face, rotating eyes glowing like two small suns, and a mean, downward-curving mouth. She'd been right!

A strong, bright-pink bolt of lightning surged from her hands straight at the rareio, which exploded into a waterfall of peppermint gloop. Paula leapt to catch the solid mask as it fell. The cold, pale-green custard splattered up her arm. The mask was as big as a real shield and it still contained a strong energy, Paula could feel it throbbing. She had to store the rareio in her cache as quickly as possible before it could regain its strength and challenge her.

'Come, dearest love,' muttered Will Carey.

'No, you come with me,' Paula snapped back. 'Fat lot of help you are.'

Paula's avatar, Lady Cora, lived in an enormous mansion on a hill. At the top of its main staircase was a locked room where she kept her cache. Breathless from riding and running up the stairs, Paula as Lady Cora took an enormous key from her skirt pockets, placed it in the lock and turned it.

The door swung open with a forbidding creak. The cache room looked like a long picture gallery, except the ornate frames on the walls were all empty. There were rows of thrones along all sides. The thrones held the sixteen enteos she'd collected so far, back behind their masks. They all turned to look at her.

She placed the latest mask on the nearest throne and it rose into the air as the space filled with the huge rareio's body. The rario seemed to understand where it was. It snarled and struggled to be free. The other enteos joined in and soon the whole room pulsated with a dark, angry energy. Paula noticed one of the frames now held a picture of the rareio, which proved she had captured something really special.

Sometimes she worried what might happen if these nasty, creepy creatures managed to escape, but that was silly: *Ray-Chay* was only a game.

5
LONELY

The whole world seemed to be playing *Ray-Chay.* At least when his dad returned Ant could play his favourite *Kismet Cosmos* undisturbed. Lia and Lance moved out, and Snoz insisted Ant take the bedroom while he took the sofa bed. Snoz had made good money driving Death Spanners around Europe. With more gigs in the pipeline, he told Ant they could start looking for a bigger place soon, one where they would both get a bedroom. And now that Lia and Lance had saved up enough money for the deposit on their flat, whenever Snoz was away on tour with Death Spanners, Ant could stay with them.

Ant often called by at Lia and Lance's flat on the way home from school. One Wednesday, after his cookery class, he took his tropical flapjacks round as a present. Wednesday was Lance's half day, so he was at home.

'You into *Ray-Chay* yet?' Lance asked through a mouthful of flapjack.

'Not really,' said Ant. 'I tried, honestly.'

'Oh ma-an,' said Lance. 'You have to give it more of a chance. It's brilliant once you get into it, I swear.'

'Are you really into it then?' Ant asked absent-mindedly. He was amazed at how well his flapjacks had turned out. He wrapped one up in a piece of kitchen roll and put it in his pocket to take home to Snoz.

'Yeah, I have to play. It's research, for work.' Lance helped himself to a third flapjack.

'Oh yeah "research". That's what you call it!' Lia said sarcastically, carrying in a pile of coursebooks, which she dumped in front of the sofa. Ant carried over a mug of the tea Lance had just made and sat on the sofa beside her.

'Hey, you've got your own suit,' said Lance. He pretended to aim a piece of flapjack at her, then popped it in his mouth at the last moment.

'I have got a boring grey suit, Ant,' Lia grinned. 'But I really fancy a zebra print one.'

'Dream on,' Lance said. 'Know what they cost?'

Lia rolled her eyes at Lance, then elbowed her little brother. 'Ant, you should give it more of a try. Lance was really kind, bringing you that suit.'

'I know, I'm sorry,' said Ant. 'I just can't see what all the fuss is about.'

'What about the b-i-i-i-g event?' Lance nodded as though he was in on some massive secret. He wasn't, Ant knew exactly what he talking about. 'You'll feel so out of it if you don't take part, mate. *Ray-Chay* in the Park. In *every* park, in hundreds of towns and cities up and down the land. It's going to be stone cold amazeballs. Live bands, street-food vans and, at three o'clock, the biggest mass *Ray-Chay* gathering. What an atmosphere! Just imagine all those thousands of people, all playing together. We've sold out of suits at the shop.'

Ant was sick of hearing about *Ray-Chay* in the Park, which was on the last weekend of the month. All his mates at school were talking about it and you couldn't switch on the telly or go online without someone hyping it up. Of course, Kody Crunch had done a new advert for it, screaming over the side of a hot-air-balloon basket as it flew over Niagara Falls. As the camera panned out, you could see that RAY-CHAY IN THE PARK was written in enormous letters across the balloon.

'Okay, I'm going to tell you something now,' said Ant. 'Have you ever heard of *Kismet Cosmos*?'

'It's a really old game, isn't it?' said Lance. 'No one plays it anymore. No one's played it in years.'

'Wrong,' said Ant. 'I do. I'm probably the last player in the whole world. And it was actually the very first VR game Kody Crunch ever made. It's what began Crunch Hut.'

'Wow, I didn't know that.'

Lia decided to chip in. 'When Dad worked at the

recycling centre years ago, someone brought in a headset with an old charger, gloves and everything. He sneaked it home for Ant. Not that anyone else would have wanted it, it was ancient even then. He's been playing it ever since.'

'The point is,' Ant said, trying to ignore the face Lia was pulling, '*Ray-Chay* is just a version of *Kismet Cosmos* and not even a very good one. It's a rip-off and no one's spotted it except me. For some reason, Kody Crunch has recycled his first ever game. Maybe he ran out of fresh ideas. I know we're all supposed to recycle more, but...'

A smile was slowly spreading across Lance's face. It stopped Ant in his tracks.

'OK, so you tried on the suit, you activated the headset and Kyto took you through some calibration movements. Then the game started and you felt you were in *Kismet Cosmos*?' said Lance.

'Yeah,' Ant nodded. Where was this going?

'You wandered about for a bit but there was nobody there except Kyto and it all seemed a bit boring?' Lance carried on.

'Yeah,' said Ant. 'Exactly.'

'Let me tell you something.' Lance leaned towards him, confidentially. 'When I put mine on, know where I am? Playing in the F.A. Cup Final at Wembley! It was boring at the start because there weren't any other players, but then the enteos showed up and it started getting good.

When Lia activates her suit, she's somewhere different from both of us.'

'The Amazon rainforest,' said Lia. 'Parkouring right up in the canopy layer. It's always been my dream to go there and see the incredible wildlife. I've read so many books about it and seen so many documentaries.'

Ant was thoroughly confused. Lance laughed, but not in a nasty way.

'The game works with you,' he explained. 'With your mind, with your memories. Most of the tech is in the front panel of the suit, beneath the Crunch Hut logo. But – and it's a big but – you know all those funny suckers inside the headset? They connect with the memory parts of your brain. Those little suckers get you to remember a place you really love and the memory becomes the setting for your game, see? *Ray-Chay* calibrates to your personal memories, just as it does to your movements. How cool is that? If you're on multiplayer, you and your friends see exactly the same enteos but you're all in different places. Everyone's virtual environment is unique. That's why it's so groundbreaking. That's exactly why people love it so much. You love *Kismet Cosmos*, so that's where the game's taken you.'

Ant's mouth dropped open. When Kody Crunch had promised his new game would change gaming forever, he hadn't been exaggerating. This was incredible, light years ahead of what any other games company was doing. But hang on: the headset was making real contact with Ant's brain? For a moment, he wasn't sure he liked the idea.

'Couldn't it be dangerous?' he asked.

'Nah!' said Lance. 'Crunch Hut spends millions on health and safety, they wouldn't market anything dangerous. The effect is temporary. When you take off the headset, it breaks the link. They've spent years testing this game on real people.'

'I didn't realise we're all playing in our own worlds,' Ant said. 'I feel like such an idiot.'

'Don't worry,' said Lance. 'Loads of people haven't worked it out yet. Kody Crunch doesn't go on about the science bit because a lot of players find it boring. They just want to be entertained. There's plenty about it on the Crunch Hut website, but people don't bother to look. Why not try it again? Once you get used to it, you'll love it, I promise. When you get to level 21 it's supposed to be amazing. No one I know has got that far, but I'm nearly there.'

That evening, Ant decided to have another go. He peered nervously at the inside of the headset but put it on anyway. Now he knew that the fizzy-head feeling was the little suckers starting to suck on his personal memories. This time he found himself on the ninety-ninth planet of *Kismet Cosmos*: planet Zoberne with its volcanoes and swamps, which is where he was in the real game. It was a brilliant copy of the planet. Ant was amazed because he hadn't realised he could remember so much detail. Zoberne was a much bigger planet than any of the others and it had taken him ages to get there. Not that he minded, he'd been really enjoying himself.

There were still no signs of life in this version of Zoberne, no Pradahl, who in the real game was now wearing a shimmering, fiery-red coat of scales. Ant's avatar Tarn was wearing armour made from the skin Pradahl had shed on the previous planet, a lapis lazuli blue.

To try and make himself feel more involved, Ant brought up the avatar menu and gave himself the name 'Tarn2'. Switching back to Zoberne, he walked around and did what Kyto the ghost monkey told him to do: he climbed up one side of a volcano, ran around the rim, then slid back down. He crashed into some lava flowers at the bottom, sending pollen bombs hurtling into the air, and Kyto made him start again. He was soon fed up. It was lonely in this familiar yet unfamiliar world without Pradahl. If he carried on, he knew the enteos would begin appearing and then he supposed it would get interesting. Yet he still felt the same way he always had. He only spent an hour each evening gaming. Why would he want to waste that time on *Ray-Chay* when what he longed to do was play the real, honest-to-goodness *Kismet Cosmos*? It didn't matter how amazing the new technology was, there was simply no comparison.

'Sorry, Lance,' Ant said, removing the headset and peeling off the suit. Not that Lance was around to hear. 'Sorry, everyone. It's just not that interesting.'

Ant knew he was going to feel more out of it than usual on Saturday when *Ray-Chay* in the Park was on. Practically everyone would be at the event. Thousands of people up and down the country, all finding enteos together. All racing, chasing, collecting and destroying. Ant would probably go to the table-tennis club. He could always tilt up one end of the table for some solo practice if there was no one else around. Or he'd play *Kismet Cosmos*, maybe solve the final puzzle path and reach the hundredth planet. He wasn't sure what would happen when he reached the hundredth planet but hoped that it didn't mean the end of the game.

Ant had always quite liked the fact he was the only one who still played *Kismet Cosmos,* but now he wished he had someone else to share it with. For the first time he realised how lonely he felt.

6

THEFT

Griff was super-excited about *Ray-Chay* in the Park except for one thing. His mum was going too.

'You can't!' wailed Griff. 'You're going to stick out in that pink suit like a … big … fat … marshmallow!'

'Griff Landsdowne,' Paula said through clenched teeth. 'Is that any way to speak to your mother? Anyway, thanks to *Ray-Chay* I've lost loads of weight, thank you very much.'

'But everyone will see you. My mates will see you.'

'So? My mates will see you, I don't go on about it!'

Griff snatched the magazine his mum had been reading off the worktop and threw it on the floor. He felt like throwing himself on top of it and beating the floor with his fists. Paula glared at him.

'Watch it, my boy, or you'll find yourself grounded this weekend. Your dad and I work our fingers to the bone for you. Without us, you wouldn't have that expensive suit. Most people can only afford the boring grey ones.'

'But Mu-um. I bet you can't even play. Not properly like me and my mates.'

Quite calmly, Paula picked the magazine up, rolled it into a tube and pointed it at Griff. 'That's all you know,' she said. 'What level are you on?'

'Level 17.'

Paula smiled. 'I've just got on to level 21.'

'Wha–?' Griff couldn't have been more surprised if she'd said she'd been picked for the Olympics.

'That's right. And the other day I called out a rareio. It's in my cache.'

'A *rareio*?'

'Yes. A rare-i-o,' she stretched out the word with glee. 'Peppermint flavour. That's what you call it. Special enteos like this one have "flavours".'

Griff didn't know what to say. His mum seemed to know a lot more about it than he did. Normally he could get Paula to do whatever he wanted, but there was something different about her, a new kind of strength. It made him nervous. His mum was almost like a rareio herself, standing there smirking, and Griff had just found out he wasn't a strong enough player to challenge her.

Without another word, Paula went out through the patio doors, strolled down the garden path, plonked herself in the chair by the fish pond and carried on reading her magazine.

Griff was fuming. How on earth had his mother managed to get to level 21? How, in heaven's name, had she got her hands on a rareio? If she was telling the truth, of course. If she wasn't telling a little mumsy-wumsy porky-pie to stun Griff into shutting up about *Ray-Chay* in the Park.

No. Griff knew his mum well enough to believe her. She had found a rareio and had it banged up in her cache. Griff felt so jealous. And embarrassed. What if his mates found out? It wasn't fair, *Ray-Chay* was supposed to be for Griff's generation! How come old people were allowed to play it? Why wasn't there an *upper* age limit on these games?

When Griff's dad came home from work, the three of them ate together. Griff was quiet, pushing the spaghetti bolognese around his plate, hatching a plan. After tea, his dad holed himself up in his study with his emails while Paula left for her pilates class. Griff felt anxious, but with the house all quiet, there seemed no better time to put his plan into action.

If he could just get to see the rareio, that would be enough. Then he could boast about it to Lyle and Boom. As rareios only appeared to the greatest players, it would prove how much better he was at playing *Ray-Chay* than they were. He could almost taste the glory!

A small, irritating voice reminded Griff that it was his mum who was actually the better player. He chose to ignore it.

How could he get to see it? Obviously, each suit would only respond to its owner, but what if he wore his own suit and tried his mum's pink headset on with it? That couldn't be dangerous, could it? The worst that could happen was that it simply wouldn't work.

Griff crept into his parents' bedroom. Why are you creeping? he asked himself. You're not going to steal anything. No, but the feeling in the pit of his stomach told him he was doing wrong.

Griff swallowed as he faced the wall of mirrored wardrobes. Searching through them really would make him feel like a thief. Then he spotted a pink reflection in the mirror. Paula's *Ray-Chay* suit was hanging behind the bedroom door, with her headset. Griff was already wearing his own suit and he put his headset on the bed. He wouldn't be needing that.

Griff unhooked the ridiculous bunny-eared headset and placed it on his head. It fitted just as tightly as his own. He was glad Lyle and Boom weren't around. He must look so weird: superhero below, Easter bunny above. Nervously, he gave the order: 'Griff. Activate!'

It took longer to load than usual and the strange fizzing in his head became horribly uncomfortable. At last, to Griff's delight, the game began. After the calibration movements, he was back in *Ray-Chay* but it wasn't the game he knew. He was outside in the dark with a starry sky above him and he was hanging on to someone riding a horse! This was all wrong. Where was the adventure play centre? He tried to let go of the rider, but nearly fell off and had to grab on to him again, sharpish.

A fork of lightning flashed across the sky and the man spoke over his shoulder in a deep voice, 'Where tonight, my lady?'

So, this was what his mum got up to when he was at school and his dad was at work!

The strange lightning flashed again as the rider turned. The bloke's masked face squashed together for a moment. Griff realised it wasn't lightning but a glitch. Was it caused by the mismatch between the headset and the suit? Maybe his mum's level 21 headset didn't appreciate being worn by a level 17 player. Griff knew he shouldn't hang around.

'I want to see my cache!' he said, trying to sound as ladylike as possible.

'Very well,' the bloke answered. The horse galloped faster.

By the time they arrived at the mansion, the glitches were worse, coming every minute or so. It was a struggle to get down from the horse, as he was wearing a massively long dress, but Griff had the strangest feeling that he knew where his mum's cache was.

Leaving the man on the horse, he waddled up the steps and pushed open the door. The hallway was splendid, with ornate mirrors reflecting warm candlelight, but he didn't have time to stop and admire it. He headed up the stairs and pulled a large, iron key from his pocket.

Did he want to do this? Did he really want to do this?

Fear gripped Griff as he turned the key in the glitching lock and rested his hand on the knob of the door.

No, he had to. He had to see what the rareio looked like. He'd take one look, that would be enough. One quick look, then he'd leave.

The enteos were sitting on thrones around the sides of the long room, like guests at the most boring party in the world. They turned when Griff walked in. To his left sat one twice as big as the others, glowing a pale, ghastly, bog-gas green. As soon as it spotted Griff, it began to pulse with a misty inner light, quite different from a normal collector. As if to hammer the point home, the one picture hanging on the gallery wall was a painting of this strange creature.

So there it was: a rareio! Not many players in the whole *Ray-Chay* universe had seen one. Weren't Lyle and Boom going to be amazed when he described it? Of course, he wouldn't be able to say *where* he'd seen it but…

The rareio and the other enteos were growing restless. They groaned as they rocked to and fro. The rareio was rocking most of all, and snarling too. Griff knew he should go but he couldn't just take off the headset. He would have to lock the room properly, or his mum might guess he'd been in there.

Then something happened. There was another glitch, a really long one this time, and when the room reappeared, it was just as before – except for one thing.

The rareio had gone. Vanished. All that was left was the shield-shaped mask, staring up at Griff from the seat of the throne. From the corner of Griff's eye, he also noticed the empty picture frame on the wall.

What Griff did next was instinctive. If he'd stopped to think, he wouldn't have dared. He darted towards the throne, picked up the mask, then ran back to the door. His hands were trembling as he locked the rest of the enteos in the room. Their howling was terrifying. His heart was hammering as, in real life, he swapped his mum's headset for his own. Within moments, feeling very dizzy, he was back in his familiar play centre world.

And he was still holding the mask! He couldn't believe it! But the mask's energy was so much stronger at level 17 than it had been at level 21. Griff's hands throbbed like they'd been stung by bees. The bones in his arms ached right up to his shoulders. He fought the temptation to drop the mask and run. Everything would be all right as long as he could get it back to his cache straight away.

But before Griff could take a single step, the rareio's body began filling out behind the mask. Within seconds, the rareio was towering over him with misty peppermint light pulsing strongly inside it like a heavy heartbeat.

'Collector!' shouted Griff, but the rareio was having none of it. Like an escaped wild animal, it seemed delighted with its new freedom, but furious at the same time. It was still very glitchy, and each time it glitched, it roared with rage and pain and glared at Griff, its eyes burning through the slits of the mask. The rareio looked like it hated Griff and it was easy to guess why. It blamed the boy for corrupting and damaging it. Griff was its enemy.

'Didn't you hear me? Collector!' shrieked Griff. He was properly scared, almost as though the rareio were threatening him in real life. What was the worst that could happen? he asked himself. Maybe his suit would deactivate for good. What were the chances of his parents buying him another suit? Zero, once his mum had found out what he'd done.

Griff couldn't see any stats floating around the rareio's head because it should not have been appearing to a level 17 player. In desperation, he clasped his hands over his heart in a double fist. A weak blue flash blurted out and died before it even reached the rareio.

From behind its mask, the rareio laughed, a horrible twisted sound. It began closing in on Griff.

Griff started backing away. For pity's sake, what was

happening? Enteos were supposed to be raced, chased, collected or destroyed; they weren't supposed to chase *you*! His lightning bolts were getting smaller and weaker and his health thermometer was on its final bar. Exhausted in real life as well as in the game, with the rareio nearly on top of him, Griff summoned up all his power for one final lightning bolt.

'Collector!' he croaked.

The smallest flicker flew from his hands. It was no bigger than the flame on a birthday cake candle. But it caught the rareio at the very moment it was glitching. To Griff's relief, the mask dropped to the floor, clattering at his feet. Out of breath, he picked it up and could feel that terrible pulsing energy again, sending tremors shooting up his arms. There was no time to waste. He bolted away to the party room where he kept his cache.

7
SLIMY CONFETTI

'Lev-el 21, I said lev-el 21!' Lance chanted, punching the air with his fists as though he'd just returned from victory at the footie.

'What's it like at level 21 then?' asked Lia. For once, she looked impressed. Turning to Ant, she said, 'You playing *Ray-Chay* yet?'

'A bit,' Ant lied, hiding behind his mug of tea. He didn't like lying but he hated feeling like he was letting Lance down. Lance had gone out of his way to bring him that suit.

Ant needn't have worried. His sister was more interested in Lance, who did one of his gymnastic dives over the back of the sofa, stretched out and began to tell them all about it. The shop had been quiet that afternoon and Daisy, his boss, had actually suggested he go and play in the back room, knowing he'd nearly reached level 21. It sounded amazing that you could get paid for playing games, but there was a practical reason. If a member of staff had in-depth knowledge of a game, he or she could do a better job of explaining it to customers.

'From level 21 onwards, it feels like a whole new game. All that racing and chasing was just about skilling up. From here on in, it's about finding new, more difficult destroyers and using your cache.' Ant had never seen Lance so animated. Suddenly the game did sound a lot more exciting. Ant wondered whether he'd been wrong about it.

'Each of the special destroyers has a matching collector the same flavour,' Lance jabbered on. 'If you've got that particular collector in your cache, you'll not only zap the destroyer but you'll gain thousands of extra points. Literally, thousands. This morning, I found one of these new destroyers up in the south stand. It was this amazing bubblegum flavour and so shiny. I knew I had the matching collector so I zoomed to the dressing room – that's where I keep my cache. I just said, "Wanna play?" and it just kind of jumped up and melted over the top of me. I felt this funny sensation starting in my head and running down my entire body.' He wiggled his fingers from his head down to his toes and shuddered.

'Urgh!' exclaimed Lia. 'I don't like the sound of that.'

'It wasn't too bad, just weird, like nothing I've ever felt before. The thing is, when it happened, I felt exactly like I did when I was your age, Ant, the time I scored the winning goal for the school football team. The memory just popped into my head and gave me this surge of super-strength. I felt invincible. It was unbelievable. I legged it back to the south stand, called out the destroyer, used my lightning bolt and KER-CHOOM!'

Ant and Lia jumped.

'That's right,' Lance whispered dramatically. 'It exploded like slimy confetti and ZAP! Two hundred thousand points, just like that.'

'Wow,' breathed Lia.

'Sounds impressive,' said Ant. 'Is this to do with those funny suckers inside the headset again?'

'Yep, I read up about it on the Crunch Hut website,' answered Lance. 'When the collector melts over the top of you, it activates a memory of a time you felt like a real winner. When you felt so brilliant, it seemed like you could take on the world. We've all had moments like that, right?'

'I guess so,' said Ant, thinking about the table-tennis match when he'd beaten the county champion.

'For me, it would be passing the interview to get on to my college course,' said Lia. Lance reached over and gave her hand a squeeze.

'The game unlocks all that emotional energy and turns it into this ... incredible fighting ability,' he explained.

'Wow,' said Ant. Who would have thought memories could be so powerful?

'Oh, and I'll tell you something else about level 21 onwards,' Lance continued, barely stopping for breath. 'If you're really, *really* lucky you might find a limited-edition collector. They're called "rareios". They're the best of the lot. Only a few have been released but I've never seen one myself. Apparently, if you've got one in your cache, you can take on this incredibly rare "Zen destroyer", if it's the matching flavour, of course. Destroy that one and you'll zap up ten levels, so they say.'

'Ten levels!' marvelled Lia.

'Yep.' Lance shook his head in wonder. 'I've never met anyone who's actually found one and I know a lot of people in the gaming community. These rareios are so strong, they only appear to the very best players.'

By an incredible stroke of luck, Paula couldn't play *Ray-Chay* for a few days because she and Evan had hired some workmen to change their en-suite and his mum never played *Ray-Chay* anywhere except the master bedroom. For the time being, Griff knew he was safe.

He told himself not to feel bad about what had happened. It had really been his mum's fault. She had no business playing a game he and his mates were into. Plus, if she hadn't made him cross, he never would have taken her rareio. Despite telling himself this over and over, he did feel bad.

Telling Boom and Lyle he'd captured a rareio, that was *sweet.* The looks on their faces were priceless.

'How Griff? You're only on level 17, same as us!'

'I don't believe it! A rareio? They're rare as hen's teeth!'

Griff merely cocked an eyebrow and tried to look cool. 'Well, you're either a top skill player or you're not, guys. What can I say?'

'Hey, I heard that this bloke who works in the games shop in the Parade took on a level 21 destroyer,' said Lyle. 'Two hundred thousand points he got! But even he hasn't seen a rareio yet. You've done amazing, Griff, mate, I can hardly believe it!'

Griff described what the rareio looked like. Lyle and Boom hung on his every word, open-mouthed. Even though they might play the same game, one player couldn't normally enter another's cache so they weren't able to see the rareio for themselves. It didn't matter – Griff gave such a detailed description, they knew he was telling the truth.

'Oh, and guess what?' said Griff. 'We don't really see one another's worlds, guys, when we play together. They're all different. What kind of world are you in?'

It took a while for Boom to understand. 'Monster truck superdrome,' he said at last, with a shrug.

'Hey, how come? My game's on a battlefield.' Lyle looked similarly confused.

'And mine's in an adventure play – I mean in space.' Griff suddenly realised how embarrassing it would be to admit what his world was. 'See, same enteos, but different worlds. We all play in worlds that mean something to us personally. The game uses our memories of our favourite-ever places. That's why *Ray-Chay* is so brilliant. Monster truck superdrome … battlefield … space.' He pointed at Boom, then Lyle, then at himself.

His friends looked puzzled.

'I mean, I LOVE space,' Griff went on quickly. 'We all know that, right? I'm always going on about space and … planets and stuff.'

'*Are* you?' Boom's face creased.

'Course I am, duh!' Griff punched Boom's arm, though not too hard.

'Oh yeah,' said Lyle. He shook his head at Boom. 'Course you are, Griff, mate. You're the biggest fan of space I ever met.'

'Anyway, I can't believe you two dummies hadn't worked it out for yourselves, about the different worlds. It's lucky I'm here, isn't it?' Griff folded his arms and waited for his friends to agree with him. He didn't have to wait long.

8

CAUGHT BY A DOLPHIN

Yet again, Ant tried getting into *Ray-Chay*. He'd got over his worries about the headset sucking on his memories. If Kody Crunch said it was safe, of course it was safe. He was sick of being the only one not playing and if it was as good in the higher levels as Lance said, it must surely be worth getting through the boring earlier levels. He also wanted to stop feeling like he was letting Lance down, because he could easily have given the suit to somebody else. Lance and Lia really wanted him to go to *Ray-Chay* in the Park with them. He wouldn't have time to get to a very high level before the event but he'd be able to take part. At least he wouldn't feel so out of it.

It didn't take long for Ant to get used to the new way of moving and he got through the first three levels quickly. He liked the fact he could feel much more in the suit than he could when wearing his usual *Kismet* headset and gloves. He found a few racers and chasers and that was pretty good fun. Pradahl had finally appeared, but this turned out to be the main disappointment.

In *Ray-Chay*, she didn't *do* anything except blow a bit of encouraging smoke. In *Kismet Cosmos*, Pradahl was feisty and quirky, always wandering off and getting into trouble. She was also fiercely loyal to Ant's avatar, Tarn. He'd spent so long training her to be the greatest dragon in the cosmos and they worked together as a team, solving puzzle paths and defeating enemies. It was odd being followed around by this boring creature who looked like Pradahl but wasn't. This dragon was just part of the scenery and there was no real point in its being there. Whenever he played *Ray-Chay*, Ant missed the real Pradahl. He loved returning to the real game and finding her there in all her wonderful, irritating glory.

At two o'clock on the last Saturday afternoon in May, all the town's Ray-Chayers flocked to Jubilee Park. For once, you couldn't play *Ray-Chay* just anywhere, for this one special day you had to be in the park. It was Kody Crunch's idea to bring people together in real life, in special community events. Hundreds of grey-suited figures were waiting eagerly, as well as a few in more expensive suits. These posh gamers cruised around like shiny sports cars, hoping to make everyone else jealous.

Ant was sitting having a picnic with Lia and Lance and enjoying people-watching. He saw Griff strutting about in his black suit like he owned the place, swishing his cape from side to side. Lyle and Boom were with him, but they looked like most people in their grey suits.

DJ Choonetto, a local radio presenter, was in the bandstand playing music while the crowd queued to buy food and drink from the vans. The atmosphere was lively and friendly and Ant was glad he'd decided to go, particularly as Lia seemed so pleased he was there.

He hadn't told Lia or Lance that in his backpack were his old headset and gloves. If the day got boring, he was going to sneak off to the Dell and play *Kismet Cosmos* instead. This was one afternoon when he wouldn't get disturbed by Griff.

A few gamers came up to talk to Lance and they all seemed super-excited. After a while, the music stopped and the crowd quietened.

'Right, people,' DJ Choonetto boomed out. 'It's a beautiful afternoon here in Jubilee Park and we're nearly ready to begin. Now, the *Ray-Chay* rules are a bit different today: you've gotta be in the park to play, obviously, and we're up against lots of other towns and cities all over the country. It's one of the biggest gaming gatherings ever and the competition's intense. Hey, but let's be positive! We can do this! Let's hear it for Westford Abbey, people!'

A massive cheer went up.

'Great, great.' DJ Choonetto quietened the crowd down again. 'Just for today, all our individual worlds have been shut down by the game's creator, Kody Crunch. Here is the man himself to tell us all about it.'

Kody Crunch's gleaming white teeth filled the big screen next to the bandstand. The shot widened to reveal the rest of him, standing in a field. 'Hey hey! There you all are! A big high five to all my Ray-Chayers in the UK,' he cried, giving everyone a virtual high five. 'What's this *Ray-Chay* in the Park all about, huh? Well, for the first time, we're all playing in the same world, the Parkworld, although we'll be able to access our caches as usual. Just remember: you might not be able to take on all the enteos, it depends what level you're at in the regular game. If you can see the stats around the enteo then get to work, otherwise leave it to someone who's on a higher level than you. The main thing is, everyone in your town is working as a team, yeah? Now, the other exciting announcement … and you're the first to find out: there's gonna be a very special "Zen destroyer" out and about today!'

There was an 'Oooo!' from the crowd and excited laughter.

'Yeah, you know you want it!' Kody pumped the air with his fist. 'I've released a real biggie and it's worth so many points, whoever destroys it probably is gonna win the contest. That's it from me. Most of all, have fun, guys!'

Kody waved with both hands and the excited crowd waved back. He then gripped handles at either side of his waist and, without warning, the jet pack strapped to his back whizzed him up into the air. They all watched until he became a small dot in the sky, then the screen went black.

DJ Choonetto piped up again. 'What a great dude that Kody is. Seriously, guys, I know not many of you will have seen a rareio yet, but if anyone here has the rareio that partners this Zen destroyer, Westford Abbey will win! Who knows?'

Ant noticed Lance exchange a fed-up face and a shrug with another gamer nearby. Clearly, neither of them had any rareios. If a brilliant player like Lance hadn't found one yet, surely nobody had.

'The time has come, people, so please spread out, make sure you have loads of room. Good luck, Westford Abbey and 3 ... 2 ... 1... *Ray-Chay*!'

Everyone gave themselves room, like in a school PE lesson, voice-activated their headsets and performed the calibration exercises. Ant was wearing his Tarn2 outfit, even though he was in the *Ray-Chay* Parkworld like everyone else. It looked a bit like the real Jubilee Park but the colours were brighter and sparklier and the bushes were sculpted into fantastic bird-like shapes: robins, eagles, swallows and owls. The edges of the park merged into wild forest. The boring Pradahl was standing beside him, worse luck. All the other gamers were dressed in skins they wore in their usual worlds. There were Romans and astronauts and spies. A football player right next to him with the name SKILLZY on his back was dribbling a ball with unbelievable skill and Ant knew it had to be Lance. Meanwhile, a spotty big cat labelled JAG22X bounded away into the distance. That had to be Lia.

A cry went up – 'CHASER!' – and suddenly everyone was running in the same direction. Ant followed as fast as he could, although of course, in real life, he was just running on the spot. The fake Pradahl flew above him as he overtook a super-bronzed surfer riding his own portable wave and the Scarecrow from *The Wizard of Oz*. He nearly crashed into a bunch of cheerleaders, but somersaulted over them at the last minute.

Ant rounded a corner and spotted the chaser, hovering in a golden bandstand at the top of a hill. Hundreds of gamers were closing in on all sides. The counting-down clock appeared at the corner of his eye: he had just under a minute to reach the chaser. He realised it was trapped in the bandstand because a dolphin had caught it in a temporary lightning bolt, just to make everything weirder.

Ant put on a spurt. He did some parkour moves over Captain Scott of the Antartic and an entire woman's football team and landed beside the dolphin with just four seconds to spare. He could see stats floating round the chaser's head.

'Hey, those were great moves,' said the dolphin.

'Thanks,' Ant replied. 'You're a strong player, holding that enteo on your own.'

'Level 25.'

'Impressive.'

The clock turned red. Ant called out 'Chaser!' and placed his double fist over his heart. The crowd around him all did the same. Hundreds of different-coloured lightning bolts shot towards the chaser. It disappeared in a puff of smoke. The clock was replaced by the scoreboard, which whirred round, adding up the points earned by everyone: 1,582!

A message flashed up in the sky, announcing that in the previous five minutes, Westford Abbey had moved up to 589th position in the whole country.

'Racer!' someone shouted but, this time, not everyone ran off immediately. Ant had to stop to get his breath back and wait for his health to rebuild. The dolphin was doing the same.

'Seriously, how do you get to be level 25?' asked Ant. He didn't mind flattering the dolphin in a friendly way.

'By being the best,' replied the dolphin, but the way she laughed told Ant she wasn't taking herself too seriously. 'No real sweat.'

'I'd be shocked if a great player like you didn't have that killer rareio,' said Ant, playing along with her.

‘I’ve got at least a hundred in my cache,’ she replied.

‘Of course you have.’

‘By the way, I like your dragon,’ said the dolphin. She pointed at the fake Pradahl, who was standing beside him again.

Ant groaned.

‘Not too helpful, huh?’

‘Iron parachute helpful,’ he said. ‘It’s just a boring version of my real dragon from another game. In the real game, her name’s Pradahl and she really is impressive. You should see her.’

‘I wish I could. She sounds good,’ said the dolphin. ‘Personally, I prefer to travel alone. And now my health has rebuilt, it’s time to go.’

‘Okay, nice chatting with you,’ he said, meaning it. He watched as the dolphin swam off through the air. She’d seemed nice.

It took Ant a little longer to recover, then he and some other players spotted a racer disappearing into the forest and ran after it. The crowd gradually broke into smaller and smaller units until there were two or three players taking on each enteo. Every five minutes, a message flashed up saying where Westford Abbey stood in the league table. Sometimes it moved up in the rankings, usually it moved down. Westford Abbey was only a small town, after all.

9

WANNA PLAY?

Before leaving the house that morning, Griff checked his cache one final time. In his play-centre world, his low-level collectors were kept in a party room with tiny tables and chairs, balloons and streamers. Among them now sat the rareio he'd taken from his mum. It glared at Griff from behind the mask and snarled and rocked on its silly plastic chair which looked like it might collapse at any moment. The rareio's picture appeared on a balloon tied to the back of the chair, which looked really silly. Griff felt embarrassed. He didn't dare go anywhere near it. After each glitch, the rareio howled as if in terrible pain. When the pain stopped, it glared at him even more furiously. It was obvious that the rareio hated Griff more and more for corrupting it. Some stats had appeared at last around its head, but they were crackly and glitchy, not like they should be. As Griff headed off to the park, he wondered whether he could ever use the rareio in the game.

In *Ray-Chay* in the Park, since everyone was playing

in the same place, instead of having to travel to your cache all the time you simply pressed a 'C' icon in the top left corner. For the first half hour after the game started, Griff didn't need to do this, not having spotted any collectors or destroyers. But he still hoped he'd get the chance to try out the rareio. Even though he was scared of it, he wanted to impress Lyle and Boom. If he could use the rareio against a destroyer, he would be a legend. Word would spread around school and soon everyone would be in total awe of him. That's why Griff insisted the three of them stick together all day. He didn't want the other two to miss his triumph.

Normally, when someone else was playing in your *Ray-Chay* world, you would see them in a skin like your own. Today, for the first time, the three friends could see one another in their usual skins. Lyle's character wore his soldier's uniform while Boom's was dressed in a tough boiler suit. Griff, on the other hand…

'What's that you're wearing?' asked Boom.

'It's a bit like a babygro,' laughed Lyle.

'It is NOT a babygro.' Griff rounded on them. 'It's what astronauts wear in the space station. Don't you know anything?' He wasn't sure if they believed him or not, but the next second, they spotted a chaser and were off again.

After catching the chaser in the forest, the scoreboard told them that Westford Abbey was currently in 918th place. 'Oh *man*!' said Griff. The three of them headed down towards a lake where, rounding a corner, they nearly collided with a highwayman and a woman in a big dress on horseback. If Griff hadn't sworn, Paula might not have realised it was him.

'Griff?' Paula, as Lady Cora, jumped down from the horse.

'Is that your mum?' said Lyle. 'It sounds just like her.'

'Hello, Mrs Landsdowne,' said Boom politely.

'Mu-um! Leave me alone,' Griff hissed. 'I'm with my mates.'

'Never mind your mates,' said Paula. 'I haven't played for days and soon as I get back on, guess what? Something's missing from my cache. Would you know anything about that?'

'What are you talking about?' said Griff, in what he hoped sounded like honest bewilderment.

'That thingy in my cache. The one I told you about.' Fortunately, Paula had forgotten the rareio's name.

'How can I get into your cache? It's impossible,' protested Griff. Lyle and Boom were looking at him suspiciously. He had to get them away.

'I am on level 21,' Paula said accusingly. 'You might have wanted to see what that was like?'

Lyle and Boom looked at one another.

'Is your mum *seriously* on level 21?' whispered Lyle.

This was turning into a disaster. 'Mu-um! As if I'd be seen dead in your suit. Anyway, it only responds to you. Shush, you're embarrassing me,' Griff said, through gritted teeth. 'Look, I'm really sorry you lost your ... whatever it was, but we've got to go. See you later.'

Griff grabbed Lyle and Boom and dragged them down the path to the lake, praying his mum wouldn't suddenly remember the rareio's name and call after him. He swatted away their questions. He was furious with her for showing him up.

A small crowd had gathered by the lakeside. The air was buzzing with excitement and Griff, Lyle and Boom pushed their way through. They'd have bumped into the Zen destroyer if it hadn't been surrounded by a thick force field.

Griff guessed immediately this was the special destroyer DJ Choonetto had been talking about. It was the most fearsome enteo he'd ever seen, a pale peppermint-green flavour, with fangs protruding from the sides of its blood-red mask.

Griff's heart leapt to his throat in excitement. He could see stats floating about the Zen destroyer's head. They were crackling and glitching a bit, but he could see them. With mounting joy and fear, he realised that he could only see these stats because he had the same flavour rareio in his cache!

The huge creature was doing what looked like tae

kwon do moves, punching and kicking its shaggy arms and legs as it rotated on the spot. The crowd gazed in fascinated horror. Nobody knew what to do. The clock in Griff's eyeline showed fifty seconds left.

'I've got it!' he whispered, hardly daring to say the words. 'I've got the matching collector! It's – it's the rareio in my cache.'

'Well, use it, buddy!' Boom squeaked in excitement.

Griff gulped. This was the moment he'd both hoped for and feared. He'd been bigging up the rareio for ages. If this didn't work, he was going to look stupid, or worse... Would it work, a level-17 player using a corrupted level-21 rareio? But, if it did work, imagine the glory! Everyone would worship him as a total hero!

There was no time for debate. They had stumbled across the special Zen destroyer. Perhaps the creature zapped from town to town and this was Westford Abbey's one and only chance to capture it. Lyle and Boom stared at Griff anxiously. Whatever he was going to do, he was going to have to do it quickly.

Griff pressed the 'C' icon and instantly found himself back in his cache. He steeled himself, stood right in front of the rareio and said, the way you were supposed to, 'Wanna play?'

The invisible chains keeping it prisoner simply melted away. The rareio rose to its blobby feet, still glitching. As it removed its mask, Griff could see a look of pure hatred on its face. Hatred for him. Nevertheless, the rareio glided towards him, rose and dissolved over the top of him. It was a really unpleasant feeling: a kind of sick shudder from head to toe.

Griff was back with the destroyer at the water's edge. The horrible feeling went away and he felt invincible. He remembered the time he'd worn a very expensive new footie strip at primary school, and everyone had been so jealous of him. He felt incredible!

The Zen destroyer stopped rotating. It clawed at the air, challenging Griff. The force field around it vanished and its stats were going wild. The clock was at five seconds.

'Destroyer!' cried Griff.

The metallic mask fell, revealing a nightmare face, all menacing eyebrows and fangs. Its eyes were wells of boiling blood.

A bolt of white lightning shot from Griff's double fist, skewering the destroyer. With only one second left on the clock, it exploded, covering the whole crowd in nauseating flob. Everyone groaned.

Through the lumpy wetness, Griff saw the scoreboard expand to fill the entire sky. Triumphant invisible trumpets filled the air as the numbers spun in a blur. They were counting down: eight hundred … six hundred … three hundred.

The crowd held its breath, spellbound.

One hundred and fifty ... one hundred ... seventy-five.

The excited buzz began again.

Forty-five ... twenty ... ten.

When it got to one, virtual fireworks exploded and the crowd went wild. Westford Abbey was in first place on the leaderboard! First place in the entire country! The main competition was over. Westford Abbey had won!

10
FROZEN

The gamers celebrated wildly. Griff the hero was getting virtual hugs from everyone, but then he felt a hard tap on his shoulder.

'So, you did have it!' his eighteenth-century mum shrieked in his face.

'Oh no, don't do this,' pleaded Griff, backing away.

'Somehow, you took that rareio out of my cache, Griff. That was the one I found the other day. You stole it, you little toad.'

The gamers nearby stopped cheering. They were listening in. Lyle and Boom looked tense.

'Mum, stop, will you? Westford Abbey's in first place. Can't you just be happy?'

'You must be joking. You are coming home with me. Take off your headset this instant.'

'Mum, I don't feel well...'

'That's not going to work with me, you sneak. You're coming home now!'

'Mum, I think I'm going to be...' He would have said

'sick' but it wasn't sickness he felt, exactly. The world was spinning like a demonic merry-go-round, but he also felt as though he was being squished from every direction at once. If he'd been able to raise his hands, he would have pulled off his headset, but in real life, his arms wouldn't move.

He started shivering uncontrollably, his teeth chattering like a machine gun. Griff looked at his mother, afraid, and dropped to his knees. The gamers standing around took several paces back and Paula gave one sharp scream.

As though Griff were attempting to pull a very tight jumper off over his head, the rareio was squeezing itself out of him. It hadn't been used up in the battle with the Zen destroyer, the way it should have been. Griff's face squished together as the tail end of the creature escaped, and he felt his body being pulled like a sausage as the rest of it worked its way out. Finally, the rareio's elongated body plopped on to the grass beside him, where it glitched uncontrollably. No one spoke, no one moved a muscle.

The rareio raised its head and looked at Griff through its metallic mask, which was back in place. It gave a hideous, hate-filled snarl, as though it wanted to kill him. It tried to rise several times, but kept dropping to its knees, panting. Griff didn't feel ill anymore, but he didn't know what to do. He was terrified.

'See!' shrieked his mother, breaking the awful silence. She pointed at the rareio with a shaky finger. 'You should never have taken it, Griff. It was too strong for you.'

The rareio lifted its head and looked at Paula. Something about the way it slowly rose to its feet suggested it recognised her. It was still glitching as it moved towards her, still glitching as she called out 'Collector!' and raised her double fist to her heart. Its awful smile stretched out beyond the edges of its mask. Paula's thunderbolt was too late. As the rareio dissolved over the top of her, it was still glitching.

'Mum!' yelled Griff. He tried to run towards her, but Lyle and Boom held him back.

'Don't be stupid,' said Boom.

'Your mum's a level-21 player. She can handle it,' said Lyle.

'But it's doing something to her. Look!' Griff stared.

Paula was frozen with her fists clasped to her chest.

Almost as quickly as it had leaped into her, the rareio leaped out again and everyone could see the difference. It was full strength now, pumped with energy and not glitching at all. It spun around to face the crowd and they all backed off.

A brave gamer dressed as Mary Queen of Scots stepped forward and cried 'Collector!' but the rareio was too quick for her. It jumped in and out of Mary Queen of Scots, leaving her frozen, absolute shock on her face.

Everything was happening so quickly. Everyone could see that the rareio was growing. After leaping into and out of another gamer, it had practically doubled in size. It wasn't leaping into everyone, it seemed to choose its victims carefully. One or two of the high-level gamers tried shooting thunderbolts at it, but they just bounced off.

'It's sucking up the gamers' power,' gasped Boom.

'I can see that,' said Griff.

'But it's only choosing really high-level players,' said Lyle. 'That's why you weren't frozen like…'

They all looked at Paula, who still hadn't moved.

'I guess they just stay like that for a few moments before they start playing again,' said Lyle. 'I think we'd better run, guys. It really hates you, Griff, anyone can see that. Come on!'

The rareio was clearly delighted with its new power. Its laughter sounded like sewage gurgling down a drain and it was literally sparkling with a nasty kind of glee. It enjoyed scaring the few players who didn't run away, chasing and clawing at them. The air was full of screams.

Griff didn't know what to do. He hated leaving his mum there, frozen. He also knew that Lyle was right. The rareio hated his guts.

'Sorry, Mum,' he called, not knowing if she could hear him or not. The three boys turned and ran.

In games, you are sometimes frozen out of the action for a while and it's no big deal. Griff was sure the effect upon his mum would be temporary. His mum was a brilliant player. He would catch up with her later and then he would give her a proper apology. When she calmed down again, she would feel proud of him because Griff had still won the whole competition for Westford Abbey. Someone would get the rareio under control and then they could all celebrate together. Griff was still the hero of the hour.

Griff didn't realise that, in real life, all around the park, Paula and the other frozen gamers were standing still as statues and no one could get a word out of them. In real life, the St John Ambulance team were already at work and an emergency call had been made to the paramedics. The sound of sirens blared in the distance, racing through traffic, as more ambulances headed straight for Jubilee Park. The nearest hospital had been warned about a major incident and were expecting casualties to arrive soon. In real life, panic was setting in.

11
REAL LIFE

Ant was glad he'd taken his backpack along, because half an hour into *Ray-Chay* in the Park, he was thoroughly bored. Perhaps it would have been different if he could have kept up with the dolphin. He'd seen her a couple of times but she was always tackling super-strength enteos. At his low level, there were very few enteos that he could take on and the novelty of watching all the other gamers charging about in their different outfits soon wore off. It was also thoroughly annoying being followed about by the fake Pradahl.

When he removed his headset, he was faced with a strange sight: all the noisy gamers jumping and running on the spot, each in their own little spaces. He was glad to see that Lance and Lia were really enjoying themselves. As he'd envisaged, Ant would easily be able to sneak off for an hour of *Kismet Cosmos* and be back before they realised he was gone. He jogged to the adventure playground, where younger kids played as usual, while their parents looked on. Ant squeezed through the gap in the railings into the Dell and took up his usual position in the small clearing on the other side of the fence.

It was such a relief to be back in *Kismet*, playing alongside his legit, wonderful Pradahl. After a particularly intense fight against a nasty pair of stingwangers, Ant paused the game and removed his headset to take a swig of water. That's when he heard the sirens, lots of them. There was something going on in the park. Snatching up his things, Ant squeezed back through the railings and ran towards the sirens.

Most of the gamers were still playing and enjoying themselves by the look of it. But some of them were standing still, frozen in odd poses. The paramedics were running towards the frozen ones. DJ Choonetto waved his hand in the face of a woman in an expensive pink costume. He was holding a bunny-eared headset that probably belonged to her. She was staring into the sky, wide-eyed and open-mouthed. Her hands were clasped over her chest in a double fist. Ant moved closer.

'Nothing,' said Choonetto, glancing at Ant. 'Not a dicky bird. I don't know if she can hear me or what? She's got a pulse and she's breathing. She's just kind of ... frozen. Statue-fied, if there is such a word.' There wasn't, but Ant could see exactly what he meant.

'How many are like this?' he asked. From where he stood, he could count seven frozen gamers, bunny woman included.

'It's hard to say. They're all over the place.'

A paramedic rushed up and patted Choonetto on the arm. 'We're going to have to stop the game,' she panted. 'We don't know what we're dealing with. They could all get struck down and there'd be too many for us to cope with. Can we stop the ones still playing and get them out of the park without creating a mass panic? Then we can see how many are ... like this.'

Choonetto and Ant ran around, persuading the gamers still playing to deactivate their suits. Word spread that something was up. There was a lot of moaning and groaning, until Choonetto ran to the bandstand and made an announcement, explaining as much as he could about what was happening. There were gasps and a few screams but Choonetto managed to quieten everyone down. He reassured friends of the frozen gamers that everything was being done to help them and it was best to leave the paramedics to do their jobs in peace. He told everyone to exit the park as quietly and calmly as possible.

Griff watched hundreds of gamers gather their belongings and head to the main gates. He couldn't see his mum among them. Yes, he'd seen her frozen, but that was only in the game. This was real life and Paula was such a strong person, she would never be one of the people going to hospital. Something else had to be wrong with those players. Paula must be among the crowd or she had left the park already, Griff kept telling himself. Even so, his heart was pounding.

Was this connected to the rareio he'd unleashed? No, that was silly. The rareio was just inside the game. Games were games. They didn't affect reality, it was impossible.

The crowd walked uneasily past the living statues. Ant caught up with Lance and Lia, who had been searching for him. His sister hugged and kissed him, hugely relieved he was all right.

'It was weird,' said Lance. 'Someone said something was happening down by the lake. Some kind of enormous rareio ran riot, apparently.'

'It's unbelievable. I heard this girl say it was jumping into people and freezing them,' said Lia. 'Wow, I'm glad I never caught one.'

'But an enteo from a game shouldn't be doing *this*,' protested Lance. 'Not freezing people in real life. This is real life, Lia!'

Ant looked around and, yes, life had suddenly become all too real. The frozen gamers could have been playing musical statues. There were far more of them than he'd first realised. Now the park was emptying, it was easier to tell.

'Twenty-nine,' one of the paramedics called to another,

as though he'd read Ant's thoughts. 'Ring the hospital and let them know.'

The first ambulance was driving out through the park gates. People stood aside to let it pass. Turning to watch it go, Ant nearly bumped into Griff, Lyle and Boom. They were too busy arguing to notice him.

'So, what? You're saying this is all my fault?' Griff was pointing back at the park.

'Yeah, but keep your voice down,' said Lyle. 'You don't want everyone knowing, stupid.'

'You're stupid,' said Griff. 'Aren't you forgetting something? I'm the one who just won *Ray-Chay* in the Park for Westford Abbey!'

'Seriously? Do you think that matters now?' Lyle rolled his eyes.

Griff looked as though he'd had all the wind knocked out of him. It took him a few moments to come back at Lyle. 'You can't blame me for what happened by the lake.'

'Hey, hold on. You've confessed you took that rareio from your mum's cache,' Boom joined in. 'Just admit it, you shouldn't have taken it. It was from level 21 while you're only level 17, same as us. You corrupted it. You turned it into the devil, you idiot. No wonder something bad's happened.'

'These people are ill, that's all. They've got some mystery virus or something. Not. My. Fault.' Griff leaned right into Boom's face.

'It's a bit of a coincidence, though,' said Lyle. 'The people frozen in real life are exactly the same ones frozen in the game after the rareio jumped into them. Like your mum, Griff.'

'No, no, not Mum.' Griff kept looking from Boom and Lyle to the park then back again. Ant saw his eyes fill with tears. 'Even if all this does have something to do with the rareio, well, I didn't know it was going to happen, did I?'

'Nobody's saying that,' Boom said. 'It's still your fault the rareio turned into that evil *thing*. You saw it, Griff. It was terrifying!'

'Both of you, keep your voices down,' Lyle hissed, 'or we'll have a lynch mob after us.'

'After him, more like.' Boom pointed at Griff.

'Shurrup!' shouted Griff, his expression miserable.

The three boys carried on snapping at each other. Ant felt an arm around his shoulder. It was Lia, steering him out of the path of another ambulance. Although he would have liked to hang about and listen in to the argument, he let himself be led away, still cradling his backpack. The mainly grey-suited crowd were walking along so quietly, it was really eerie.

'Come on,' Lia whispered in his ear. 'I've texted Dad to let him know we're okay. Let's go back to our flat. We can turn on the news and find out what's going on.'

12
INVESTIGATORS

The next few days were weird.

Kody Crunch made a short film which was soon all over the internet. The whole world was following what was happening in Westford Abbey. In the film, for once, Kody wasn't lounging on his yacht or parachuting into view. He was sitting in a leather armchair in a sombre-looking room. He didn't once flash his smile, or his finger pistols. It was strange to see him with his large, white teeth tucked away in his mouth and his hands folded in his lap, though he still wore his sunglasses, as if he could not do without them.

'From the bottom of my heart, I want to say sorry for what's happened to *Ray-Chay*,' said Kody. 'That's why I've sent my experts over to the U.K. to investigate exactly what's gone wrong. If there's anything I can do, anything at all, then I shall do it, I give you my word. My heart goes out to those brave players, lying there in hospital, and to their families and friends. I am receiving hourly updates. Thank you and bless you all.' Just before the screen faded, he reached beneath his sunglasses to wipe away a tear.

Even though the frozen gamers were in hospital, the gates of Jubilee Park remained padlocked, with signs warning the public to keep out. All the *Ray-Chay* worlds in the country were shut down except for the Westford Abbey Parkworld and only the Crunch Hut investigators were allowed in to play. Although the police were out and about, they seemed content to trust Kody's investigators, who were working in the park around the clock, playing the game and trying to find out what had gone wrong.

The doctors at the hospital had never seen anything like it. It was like no coma they'd seen before. In all the tests, the gamers seemed fit and healthy, but they were stuck in these strange frozen positions, even when put to lie down in bed. They all wore identical expressions of surprise, with their eyes and mouths wide open. They didn't communicate in any way, not even a blink. It was as though time was standing still.

The whole gaming community was horrified. Ant found out all he could from Lance, who learned a lot from people who came into the games shop. Witnesses who'd seen the rareio said it had only leaped into high-level players. Each time, it had grown bigger and stronger. There was lots of coverage of the story in the media and it didn't take long for Boom to blab about how Griff had stolen the rareio from his mother's cache. Gaming experts speculated that the theft had corrupted the rareio, making it extremely unstable and dangerous. Somehow, the corrupted rareio had stunned the high-level players, sucking up their gaming power and freezing them in the same moment.

There was simply no waking them. Removing their headsets and suits did no good. Experts suspected that part of the rareio's corrupted code had somehow crossed the interface between human and machine and infected the players' brains. Even though they weren't playing, they were still linked to the rareio. If this were true, destroying the rareio might be the only way to break that link and wake them up.

The trouble was, even though the Crunch Hut investigators were exceptional players, the rareio was too strong even for them. From time to time, they would give interviews to journalists, detailing the long, drawn-out battle. The rareio was fighting back ferociously. It was trying to leap into the investigators, but so far they had been quick enough to dodge it, while trying to launch their own attacks. It was a stalemate.

Ant always stopped outside the park gates on his way to and from school. Sometimes he caught sight of the investigators at work. From what he could see, they didn't seem to be battling *that* hard. Most of the time, they were just standing around, which seemed peculiar.

If only, Ant thought. *If only I could get into Ray-Chay with the real Pradahl.*

Ant couldn't help wondering if more could be done. The investigators didn't seem strong enough to defeat the rareio. Even though he wasn't an expert at *Ray-Chay*, he believed in the strength of his *Kismet Cosmos* dragon. If anyone could take on the rareio, it was Pradahl. She had loads of special moves, and phenomenal items in her inventory which he'd been saving up. Because *Kismet Cosmos* and *Ray-Chay* were both Crunch Hut games, it was possible they'd been built with the same game engine. Perhaps there was some way of getting Pradahl into *Ray-Chay*?

Yet there was that padlock on the gates and the investigators were actively discouraging all offers of help. Warnings had gone out: any players who got caught in the Parkworld would find themselves in ten tons of trouble.

When Griff realised that his mother's frozen state wasn't just temporary, his world collapsed.

He should never have stolen the rareio from his mum's cache – that was *wrong*.

He should never have boasted about it to Lyle and Boom or prided himself on being such an amazing player – he wasn't.

Most of all, he should have spotted the warning signs that he'd corrupted the rareio: the glitching, the look of pure evil on its face. He should have realised the danger and not used the rareio in the game. At the time, all he had been able to think about was being a hero and winning the game for Westford Abbey.

And now his mum was in hospital. No one could say if she was ever going to get better.

Griff spoke to the doctors and then the investigators and in a small, guilty voice gave them all the information he could about the rareio and how he'd taken it from Paula's cache. He answered their questions honestly. He hoped desperately that they'd find some way of unfreezing all twenty-nine '*Ray-Chay* Victims', as the newspapers were calling them. The investigators assured Griff and his dad that they were doing all they could to destroy the rareio. Once they did that, they hoped Paula and the others would wake up.

Ant couldn't help but feel sorry for Griff, who wasn't exactly Mr Popular anymore. The kids at school avoided him. Lyle and Boom wanted nothing to do with him. He spent most of his time on his own.

Ant had had to learn how to stay in control of his gaming. That's why he and his dad had come up with the one-hour/two-hour rule. For Griff to go behind his mum's back and steal from her cache, he'd been letting the game control him. That's how Ant saw it.

One Friday lunchtime, Ant broke away from his friends and went over to Griff, who was sitting in a corner of the tennis court looking thoroughly miserable.

'You okay?' asked Ant.

Griff glanced at him and frowned. 'Like you care.'

'If I didn't care, I wouldn't ask.'

Griff glared straight at him. 'Okay, if you want to know, I'm feeling rubbish. My mum's still in hospital, I don't know how long for. Everyone hates me. *I* hate me and everything's … everything's gone wrong…'

Ant heard the sob in Griff's throat. He turned his head so as not to embarrass him.

'Griff, how did you get hold of the rareio in the first place?'

'Why? So you can hate me even more?' said Griff.

'I might be able to help.'

Griff wiped his nose on the back of his hand. 'Help? *How*?'

'I've had an idea.' Ant crouched a few feet from Griff, his back against the wire fence. 'This happened because you did something you shouldn't have been able to do. You went into someone else's cache.'

'And…?' Griff was starting to sound annoyed.

'That should be the starting point for any investigation. You explained this to the Crunch Hut guys?'

'Course I did! I want my mum out of hospital. I want everyone out of there. I told the investigators everything I could. Honestly, everything.'

'And what did they say?'

'Not a lot.' Griff shrugged.

Ant got to his feet and paced up and down. 'It feels like they're missing something. I pass the park gates every day and … I don't know … when I see the investigators, they don't seem to be *doing* much. They're not fighting, they're just standing around. Tell me, Griff, how exactly *did* you get into your mum's cache?'

'Do I have to go through it all again?'

'Please?' said Ant. 'Just tell me.'

'All right, if you must know, I put her headset on. I was wearing *my Ray-Chay* suit but I put on *her* stupid headset. That's all. Suddenly I wasn't in my world, I was in hers. I could get into her cache. I could go anywhere. Not properly, it was all glitchy. I knew there was something wrong. I should have stopped there and then.'

Ant sat down in front of Griff. 'Tell me exactly what happened,' he said, trying to control his mounting excitement. 'Start at the beginning. Don't leave anything out.'

By the end of lunch break, Griff had told Ant everything and a plan was hatching in Ant's brain.

'I need you to meet me after school,' he said as the bell rang. 'Go home, get your *Ray-Chay* suit and headset and meet me in the Dell at four. The same place you found me playing that time. Don't tell anyone.'

'There's no one to tell,' said Griff. 'No one's talking to me, remember? Anyway, we're not supposed to play *Ray-Chay*. Not any more…'

'I know but I've had an idea and if it works, it might help. I don't want to build up your hopes but … it might.'

'Why do you want to help me? We've never exactly got on.'

Ant was already walking towards the school buildings as Griff called after him. He stopped. 'I know,' he said over his shoulder. 'You're an idiot, Griff. You're spoilt, you're annoying and I've never liked you. But I can't stand by and watch you suffer.'

Griff's mouth snapped shut and Ant headed off to his next lesson.

Griff knew nothing about Ant's mum, Carol. She had become very ill and died when he was just three years old, but he still remembered her kindness, her sense of fun and her beautiful smile. There were photos in their old album of her building sandcastles with Ant and Lia on the beach and snuggling up with them on the sofa to read a story. They still had the same sofa at home. Even though it made them cry sometimes, Snoz often talked about Carol, telling Ant and Lia how proud she would be to see them growing up so brilliantly.

Ant felt sorry for Griff. If there was any way he could help get the boy's mother back to him, he was determined to do it.

13
BACK IN THE PARKWORLD

Ant decided not to talk to the Crunch Hut investigators. If he told them his idea, he was afraid they might want to try it for themselves and one thing was for sure: he would never let anyone, *anyone*, mess about with Pradahl. He knew he'd be putting himself at risk, though, which is why he needed Griff as back-up. He had no one else to ask and he guessed Griff would do pretty much anything for his mum. If what he'd heard was true, the rareio wouldn't be interested in a low-level player like Griff, but it was just possible that it would be interested in a *Kismet Cosmos* player who'd reached the ninety-ninth world.

The idea might not work at all. Even if they were built with the same game engine, *Ray-Chay* and *Kismet Cosmos* were very different games.

Griff was late. Ant had nearly given up on him when he came hurtling down the overgrown track from the Parade with his bulging backpack slung over one shoulder. 'I've got to get home by quarter to five or my dad's going to lose it,' he panted. 'We're going to visit Mum at the hospital.'

'How is she?' asked Ant.

'The same.'

Griff glared at Ant suspiciously. Ant said nothing. He just pulled his grey *Ray-Chay* suit out of his backpack and changed into it quickly. Griff put his on too. 'What now?' he said.

'Okay, I think we're close enough to the park to try getting into the game.' Ant took a deep breath. 'But with one difference. I'm going to wear this…' He pulled his *Kismet Cosmos* headset from his backpack.

'You're kidding,' groaned Griff. 'That's your idea? Seriously? I mean … *seriously*?'

'I know you weren't impressed with *Kismet Cosmos* when you tried it, but that's because I'd set it in flat-map mode,' Ant said, keeping his cool. 'That's not how it is normally. *Kismet* is an amazing game, even if I am the only one who still plays. I've been training my ace dragon up for months. Years. Her name's Pradahl. She's really powerful.'

'But there are no suckers in your *Kismet* headset. It looks completely different. It won't work,' said Griff.

'If we were playing the game normally, true.' Ant pressed on. 'But this is *Ray-Chay* in the Park. It doesn't use the memory technology with those sucker things. We're all playing in the same world for once.'

'You've really thought about this, haven't you?' Griff looked more interested. 'Do you really think your dragon could beat the rareio?'

'If I can get her into the *Ray-Chay* world, yes, I think she could. You wore your mum's headset with a different suit, didn't you? I'm guessing my suit might work with the *Kismet* headset. It'll even plug into the suit with the same cable, I've tried it. It's a bit of a long shot, but they're both Crunch Hut games. Most of the tech that runs *Ray-Chay* is in the front panel of the suit. *Ray-Chay* would be the dominant game, but Pradahl's so strong, she might be able to get in.'

'But what if there's glitching?' said Griff. 'I told you what happened when I wore my mum's headset. That's what made everyone ill.'

'If there is glitching and it gets too bad, we'll stop,' said Ant. 'I can't promise this is going to work, Griff, but it's got to be worth a try?'

Griff sighed but nodded. 'What do you want me to do?'

'Back me up,' said Ant. 'The rareio won't be interested in you – you're not a high-enough level – but in *Kismet Cosmos* I'm, like, on the ninety-ninth planet. That's massively high.'

Griff whistled. 'It hates me though,' he muttered to himself. 'It really hates me.'

'What?'

'Nothing.' Griff looked away.

'If something goes wrong,' Ant continued. 'If the rareio – you know – *gets* me, freezes me, you'll have to go for help.'

'In real life?'

'In real life.'

Griff swallowed. 'Okay.'

Ant paused before putting on the *Kismet* headset. 'Oh, one last thing. The investigators are in the Parkworld playing right now. We can't let them see us in the game, okay?'

'They'd be mad we got back in, right?'

'Yeah,' said Ant. 'But also, I really want to see what they're up to.'

Ant flicked the switch on his headset and for a few moments he didn't think his plan was going to work. There were distant sounds and misty patches of light but that was all. Little by little, his vision began to clear and his heart leaped as he realised he'd made it: after the usual calibration sequence, there he was, back in the *Ray-Chay* Parkworld with its dazzling colours and fantastic bird-shaped bushes.

He looked down at himself. Something about the way his outfit shone convinced him he was playing as his original Tarn avatar. He felt something nudge his shoulder and, turning, came face to face with Pradahl. She was in!

She was the real, legit Pradahl. He could tell by her curious expression as she looked around at the strange new world and the way she butted her head against his shoulder. She was as pleased to see him as he was to see her. Ant pressed the shining scale in the middle of her chest to call up her inventory and make sure he could get at her items. He could.

So far, Ant's plan was working.

Griff, aka YoBullit, was standing a little way off, at the edge of the lake. Ant was surprised to see his babygro but didn't say anything. There hadn't been any glitching yet, which was encouraging. Perhaps his *Ray-Chay* suit recognised his genuine high-level *Kismet* status, so the two bits of equipment felt at ease with each other? He didn't have time to dwell on this, he had to get going.

Ant ran over to Griff. 'This isn't a game anymore,' he said, 'so let's forget our avatar names. If we call each other "Tarn" and "YoBullit" it'll just feel like we're playing. We've got to take it seriously, so you're still Griff and I'm still Ant.'

'Except no real names in front of the investigators,' said Griff. 'If they catch us.'

'Yeah. We'll be Tarn and YoBullit in front of those guys.' They nodded at each other, then headed round the lake, Prahdal following.

Griff stopped. 'Here's where I caught the rareio,' he said sadly. 'And here's where it caught my mum.'

'Well, it's not here now,' said Ant. 'Let's keep under the bushes as much as we can. We mustn't be seen.'

Ant went first, followed by Pradahl, then Griff. Luckily, Pradahl wasn't a huge dragon, especially when her wings were small, when she didn't need to fly. They crept through the shadow of the bushes, then headed up the steep path to the main part of the park. The rareio could be anywhere. Wherever it was, the investigators were bound to be there too.

Halfway up, they heard clanging and angry voices. Ant made a signal and the three of them hid in a cluster of bushes trimmed to look like peacocks with their tails spread wide.

'I'll go and see what's happening,' Ant whispered. 'Wait here. No, Pradahl – stay. I won't be long.'

Pradahl looked uncertain but Griff stroked her nose gently and she agreed to wait.

Ant followed the path zig-zagging up to the golden bandstand. He edged out of the bushes to get a better look.

Shading his eyes from the intense sunlight, he could see the peppermint-coloured rareio filling the bandstand. Its face had grown so big, the mask was barely covering its nose. It wasn't happy at all. Its great fists were wrapped around the metal posts of the bandstand. The clanging they'd heard was the sound of the posts shaking. New posts had been added in the usual gaps to trap it. When it shook them, the whole bandstand shook.

Ant could see the investigators. Together, it should have been easy for them to destroy the imprisoned rareio, but they didn't even seem to be trying. The investigators' avatars looked identical: all wore white suits with a green stripe running up each side and grey helmets. One of the investigators was poking the rareio with a long, thin stick with a twist at the end. It seemed to be giving it electric shocks and making it angry. Another investigator appeared to be studying the stats around its head. A third was standing guard a little further away, holding a similar stick to the first.

Ant waited until the guard's back was turned and ran across the small grassy clearing, keeping low to the ground, careful not to make a sound. He reached another row of bushes, clipped to look like a row of pigeons marching up the hill. He crept between the pigeons' legs and approached the bandstand slowly. He stopped when he was as near as he dared go. From here, he could hear what the investigators were saying.

14

OPERATION WIPEOUT

'How much longer do we have to keep doing this?' asked the investigator, prodding the rareio with her weapon. Each time bolts of lightning flew out of the twisty end, the rareio flew into a rage and rattled the bars of its cage ferociously.

'As long as it takes,' said the one studying the stats, who seemed like the boss. Ant thought there was something strangely familiar about his voice. 'Until we find out what exactly went wrong, so it won't happen again. We were so close, *so close* to success with Operation Wipeout. If that stupid kid hadn't taken the rareio from his mother's cache...'

'I suppose it did show us there's a problem with the game,' said the prodder, who was probably his deputy.

The boss ignored her.

'What about the frozen gamers?' asked the guard. 'We'll to have to destroy this thing soon or they'll never wake up.'

'No way,' said the boss. 'Not until we get answers. If

that means removing it from the *Ray-Chay* game and putting it somewhere else, fine. That might be better. We'll tell everyone *Ray-Chay* is fixed and then they can carry on playing. But we can't destroy this rario. Not yet.'

'Where would we put it?' asked the guard.

'We could transfer it to some old Crunch Hut game. Something nobody's played in years,' said the boss.

'*Kismet Cosmos*?' suggested the deputy.

'Yeah,' the boss chuckled. 'Actually, that would be kind of sweet.'

Ant felt his stomach churn. How dare these investigators think of turning this monster loose in *Kismet Cosmos*, his favourite game in the whole world? He felt sick. He felt like screaming insults at them, but managed to control himself. He had to focus on what they were saying.

'It could take years to find out what went wrong,' said the guard. 'I can't help feeling sorry for all those frozen gamers and their families. They think we're trying to kill it.'

Without warning, the boss flipped out. 'Sorry? Sorry! Do you know how many years I've spent working on Operation Wipeout? Do you know how much money I stand to lose? Some kid goes and shmucks it all up and I'm supposed to be like, "Hey, never mind?"'

'I'm sorry, Kody,' said the guard.

Kody? Ant shuddered as he realised where he'd heard the boss's voice before. Could he really be standing within a few metres of *the* Kody Crunch?

Kody hadn't finished having a go at the guard. 'Get this into your thick skull!' He sounded genuinely angry. 'Those frozen gamers can stay frozen for eternity for all I care. Finding out what happened to my rareio and saving Operation Wipeout, *that's* what matters. Have you got that?'

Ant could hardly believe his ears. Was this the same Kody Crunch who'd wiped away a tear and promised he'd do everything possible to help the frozen gamers? Was this the same coding genius Ant had always looked up to? As he tried to take in what he'd heard, Ant felt disappointment, shock, anger. Most of all, he felt cheated.

Before he had a chance to think what he should do, Ant felt a tap on his shoulder. Turning, he came face to face with the dolphin he'd met during *Ray-Chay* in the Park. It was a weird echo of their first meeting, when she'd captured the first chaser in the same golden bandstand.

'What are you doing here?' whispered Ant.

'I could ask you the same question!' whispered the dolphin. 'I'm level 25 in *Ray-Chay*. I could take on the rareio. At least I'm willing to try...'

'That's great,' whispered Ant, 'but there's something you need to know.'

It was obvious that the dolphin hadn't heard what he'd

just heard. It was just as obvious that she wasn't remotely interested in listening to Ant.

'The other day you asked me how I got to be level 25?' the dolphin whispered. 'Okay, I have done plenty of level-grinding, slogging away to build up points, but basically, I just love the game. I want to see everything return to normal so we can play *Ray-Chay* again. Oh, and of course I want to help those frozen gamers. I'm ready to put my skills to the test and defeat that thing. I just know I can do it!'

'Wait. Hold on a moment. I've got to tell you something,' whispered Ant, but the dolphin was too pumped up to listen. Its eyes were shining and it was wiggling from side to side, getting ready to jump out and surprise the investigators. Ant persisted, 'Those guys don't want to destroy it. That's what they've told everyone but really they're just studying it to find out what went wrong. Do you see the boss, the guy in the middle? Can you guess who that actually is?'

The dolphin still wasn't listening. Nothing was going to stop it from doing what it had come to do. Without saying another word, it leaped from the bushes, catching the guard by surprise.

'Who are you?' The guard aimed his lightning-rod weapon at the dolphin, who raised its fins as though surrendering.

'I'm here to help,' said the dolphin. 'I'm a level-25 player in *Ray-Chay*. I could take on the rareio. I know it's dangerous but I want to have a go.'

'Sorry, buddy, you just got yourself banned.' The guard turned a dial on his lightning rod and zapped the dolphin. It disappeared immediately.

More anger bubbled up inside Ant, but he had to keep a lid on it. You've got to be bigger than the game, that's what Ant had to hang on to now. He had to concentrate. Banning a level-25 player for nothing was just the tip of this *Titanic*-wrecking iceberg.

Dealing with the rareio was going to be a lot harder than he'd imagined. It also meant taking on Kody Crunch, a total hypocrite who wasn't the slightest bit interested in saving the frozen gamers. And overshadowing all this was something called Operation Wipeout.

Ant crept back to Pradahl and Griff and told them what he'd just heard. Griff was furious and just managed to stop himself rushing up the hill to confront Kody Crunch. How could Kody do this? How could he leave Griff's mum lying there in hospital for a single second longer than he had to?

'We daren't show ourselves yet.' Ant held Griff back. 'We'd get banned straight away, just like the dolphin. That'd be it.'

'What can we do?' Griff looked tearful. 'I've got to save

my mum and the others. How are we going to destroy the rareio when Kody Crunch is actually *protecting* it? It's unbelievable!'

'We need to get it out of the bandstand somehow,' Ant decided. 'Then Pradahl can attack it from the sky. She can use all her special moves when she's in the air. One thing's for sure, Griff: whatever we try, we're only going to get one shot at it. We have to stay cool!'

Griff nodded reluctantly. 'What about coming back at night when Kody and the others have gone home?'

'No good.' Ant shook his head. 'Lance told me there are Crunch Hut investigators here all the time. When one team finishes, another takes over. Maybe *he's* not here the whole time, but they'll all be following his plan.'

'Then what about waiting till they transfer the rareio to *Kismet Cosmos*?' pleaded Griff. 'It might be easier to attack it there.'

Ant took a deep breath. He was trying not to blurt out that he didn't want his favourite game wrecked, because that wasn't the most important issue. 'If they did transfer the rareio to *Kismet Cosmos*,' he said, 'Kismet's a big place. How would you fancy searching ninety-nine-plus planets? It could take months to find the rareio and by that time...'

He didn't finish the sentence but Griff nodded. By that time, the frozen gamers could be in a worse state than they were now. Whatever they were going to do, they had to do it soon. If they came back tomorrow, the rareio might be gone.

'Plus I really want to find out what this mysterious Operation Wipeout is, and the sooner we do that the better,' Ant carried on. 'There could be something very big going down here. It's clearly something Kody doesn't want anyone knowing about. There's no point us running to the police or the newspapers because he'll only deny it. It's down to us, Griff. Like I say, first things first: we must get the rareio out into the open.'

They stood and thought. Suddenly, Griff looked excited. 'I know I'm a low-level player, so the rareio isn't likely to want to jump into me and freeze me,' he said. 'But it hates the sight of me. Anger seems to give it strength. It absolutely detests me. If it saw me right now, it would flip out completely.'

'And break out of the bandstand!' Ant stared delightedly at Griff. 'It's our only hope! First of all, we'll have to distract Kody and the others and get them away from the rareio. Right, listen carefully…'

15
BATTLE

There was a rustling in the owl-shaped bushes behind the golden bandstand. It sounded as if the owls had come to life and were starting to fly.

'Not another hero,' groaned the deputy.

'What's that noise?' the guard called over.

'Someone else must have got in, wanting to try their luck with the rareio. What's the matter with these people?' she sighed.

'Okay.' Kody Crunch pulled a small rod from his belt and extended it. He called to the guard, 'You stay here and keep watch, we'll go ban whoever it is. Shouldn't take long.'

Kody and his deputy strode off into the bushes. The guard continued pacing backwards and forwards, brandishing his lightning rod. The rareio carried on clanging and bashing about in its cage.

'Hey, give it a rest, can't you?' shouted the guard.

Suddenly the rareio started roaring at the top of its voice and shaking the cage so violently a couple of the posts came loose from the base. It was staring into the distance in intense fury, as though it could see something that made its peppermint blood boil.

The guard peered towards the bushes at the bottom of the hill. They were shaped like giant woodpeckers and eagles. He could see a face, popping in and out of the leaves. The guard began to run down towards it, but stopped. He remembered he was supposed to stay with the rareio. When he turned to run back, a terrible sight met his eyes.

The rareio had rocked about so much, the front half of the bandstand had detached from its base.

The guard approached slowly. 'Calm down, boy!' he soothed, as though speaking to his pet dog.

The rareio didn't calm down.

Uncertainly, he gave it a quick blast with his lightning rod, to show it who was master. This only enraged the beast even more. Before the guard could cry for help, the bandstand cage shattered into pieces and the rareio leaped out. It was much bigger than it had seemed squashed inside the cage.

The guard was hit by a flying post and fell back on to the grass, dropping his weapon. Kody and his deputy came running out of the owl-shaped bushes.

'What did I tell you, you idiot?' Kody roared at the stricken guard.

He brandished his lightning rod like a sword. As the

rareio closed in on the guard writhing on the ground, Kody and his deputy used their rods to draw the bars of a new cage around it. As quickly as they formed in the air, the drawings solidified into real posts.

The rareio dodged back and fore to avoid getting trapped again. Its temper now was right off the scale. Everything was happening so fast.

Ant and Pradahl watched from their hiding place in the owl bushes, where they'd been rustling the branches to draw Kody and his deputy away. Ant wondered why they didn't just get out of the game, and then realised that if Kody and the other two tried to deactivate their headsets to escape, there'd be the usual small lag. That would leave the three of them vulnerable to the rareio jumping into them and freezing them.

Ant decided to send Pradahl into battle. If the rareio became trapped again, their chance to attack would be lost.

He pressed Pradahl's shining scale to select three items from her inventory, the maximum number for one attack. Tarn had collected all these items on different planets. Ant chose a dazzle bubble from planet Parnazza, a humungobean from planet Xylo and a devil scale from planet Berowne. Each item would work for a minute before expiring and he timed them to activate as soon as Pradahl began her attack.

Preparing herself, Pradahl grew her wings to their

maximum extent ready for battle. She rose into the sky with a leathery beating of wings and began raining fire down on the rareio.

Kody cried out in shock.

The rareio's mask dropped to the ground with a clang, revealing a face full of evil. It swiped at Pradahl as she swooped to attack it again and again. Within seconds, the dazzle bubble began to work. Pradahl's scales glowed so brightly it was impossible to look at her. Neither the rareio nor Kody and his team could take effective aim as she flew overhead, pelting them with fireballs.

Ant seized his chance to run out, race across and snatch up the guard's lightning rod.

Griff emerged from the bushes at the bottom of the hill. His part of the plan had worked – he'd provoked the rareio into breaking out of the bandstand cage. Even so, it was scary to see how much the beast hated him. He raced up the hill to join Ant and Pradahl. They'd already agreed that Griff would act as a distraction, allowing Ant to defend Pradahl as much as he could while she attacked.

It took Ant a few seconds to find out how the lightning rod worked, but then he managed to give Kody and his deputy a few well-aimed zaps. Meanwhile Griff danced around, working the rareio up into even more of a fury and distracting it from Pradahl.

Kody and his deputy had been caught by surprise and didn't have their own battle plan. They turned between the rareio and the newcomers as if baffled.

As soon as the dazzle bubble gave out, the second item kicked in. The humungobean made Pradahl grow to seven times her normal size and she towered over the rareio, her fast, flapping wings strobing the sunlight. She started spitting out fireballs the size of witches' cauldrons and for the first time the rareio began to back away.

Kody Crunch was screaming orders at his deputy to run around and cage the beast from the other side, but the deputy couldn't get anywhere near.

Once the humungobean's minute was up, it was the turn of the devil scale. This was one of the deadliest items in the whole of *Kismet Cosmos* and Ant hoped it would bring the battle to a close. Pradahl shrank back to her normal size but something very strange began to happen to her fireballs.

'Watch out! They're alive!' yelled the deputy.

As soon as a fireball hit the ground, it turned into a little demon. Hundreds of them now jumped on to the rareio and skewered it with red-hot, needle-sharp horns. Soon the rareio was smothered in a sea of tiny creatures, hurling themselves at it head first, puncturing its slimy skin and clinging on like leeches. They were sucking up the rareio's energy and it was using what little it had left trying desperately to flick them off. The rareio was howling with rage as though it knew it didn't have long left.

Somehow the rareio hung on. It was still alive when the devil scale minute finished and Pradahl's fireballs became normal again. Bruised and bleeding peppermint goo, it raised itself from the ground and all the hatred in the world could be heard in its snarl. Griff was reminded of how it had looked after forcing its way out of him beside the lake during *Ray-Chay* in the Park. He felt a chill.

Ant watched as Pradahl swept down to attack, but now the items' special powers had run out, she looked more like an ordinary and fairly small dragon again. She used her best moves, including her whip tail and sideways zap, but after all the frantic attacking, he could see she was getting tired. While she was in the air, he couldn't reach her shining scale to rebuild her strength and give her fresh weapons.

'Cage the rareio! Cage it!' Kody screamed at the deputy.

He tried to attack Pradahl, but Ant zapped him. Everyone was attacking everyone again. Kody worked his way between the rareio and Pradahl and, focused on the dragon, turned his back on the beast he'd created. Immediately the rareio seized its chance.

Summoning up its last bit of strength, it jumped in and out of Kody, freezing him and giving itself an immediate and massive power surge. Swelling in size, the rareio surprised Pradahl, lungeing at her and knocking her to the floor. Pradahl reared up on her back legs, a blaze of scarlet and smoke. She screeched and came at the rareio with her yellow eyes ablaze, her wings spread wide and her tongue lashing out like a whip.

The rareio had no weapon, but each time it made contact with Pradahl, it seemed to suck strength from her. Ant could see crackling in the air, like static electricity leaping between them. Flames still burst from the dragon, doing serious damage when they struck, but they were taking longer to recharge.

The guard had retreated to the edge of the owl-shaped bushes. The deputy was trying to cage the rareio and stop Pradahl injuring it. She turned to take aim at Pradahl and the rareio leaped into her and froze her too. The rareio gave a vile, vicious laugh as it grew again. Now it was double the size it had been in the bandstand.

With Kody and his deputy out of action, it was more or less a straight fight between the rareio and Pradahl, with some assistance from Ant. Having re-energised itself with the power of two high-level players, the rareio looked massive and invincible. It struck at Pradahl relentlessly and Ant could tell that producing her fireballs was taking her more effort, yet she kept on going. Ant joined in the attack, zapping the rareio with the guard's lightning rod, but this seemed to just tickle the creature.

'Don't give up Pradahl, you can do it!' yelled Ant.

The lightning rod wasn't helping and he tossed it to Griff, who ran to the bushes and, after figuring out the controls, began drawing a cage around the guard, who was slouched in a daze on the grass.

Ant hadn't thought to use the *Ray-Chay* double fist technique. Now he tried it and to his delight a strong, red *Kismet-Cosmos*-ninety-ninth-planet-strength lightning bolt shot from his chest. It hit the back of the rareio, who stumbled forwards.

'Pradahl! Three, two, one and go!' shouted Ant.

Pradahl knew exactly what he meant: whenever they had to attack simultaneously, Ant always counted them in like this.

Ant breathed and focused all his energy on the small tunnel between his fists. This was it, the best chance of attacking the rareio that they were going to get. It had to work.

'Three … two … one … go!'

An enormous bolt of red lightning shot from his hands, just as the biggest flame-stream poured from Pradahl's nose and mouth like a waterfall of fire.

The rareio was hit from either side and it let out a roar of boiled agony, cut short by an almighty, wet explosion. Plumes of minty-coloured goo rained down across the park, over the bird bushes and down as far as the lake. Due to the incredible size of the rareio, the goo-rain seemed to go on for ages. It was drippy and sticky but smelled tinglingly fresh, like toothpaste.

Griff started to whoop with joy.

For a moment, Ant couldn't move. Even with the minty, custardy stuff dribbling down his cheeks, he could hardly dare believe that they had managed to destroy the rareio. He turned to Griff and saw the guard crouching beside him in a cage.

'Pradahl!' said Ant, beckoning her.

Kody and his deputy were rising shakily to their knees but they looked stunned, as if they didn't know where they were. If Ant and Griff were going to get some answers about Operation Wipeout, they'd have to question the guard before the other two realised.

16

RUBIE

Griff was still adding more and more bars to the guard's cage, whooping excitedly now the main trouble seemed to be over. He stopped as Ant leaned over the guard. Pradahl was flying behind Ant, framed by bright sunlight. The guard squinted up at them. He looked shaken and too scared to fight back.

'You've seen what my dragon can do,' said Ant. 'You'd better answer my question. Operation Wipeout: what is it?'

'I can't tell you,' whispered the guard.

'Oh yes, you can,' Ant said, with as much menace as he could manage. 'Quickly or I'll set Pradahl on you.'

Pradahl was still puffing smoke left over from her final attack upon the rareio. It made her look awe-inspiringly fearsome, like some hellish steam engine.

'All right. Just don't say I told you,' whimpered the guard. 'Operation Wipeout is a way Kody Crunch has found to control people. It happens when a rareio jumps into you…'

'SHUT UP!' Kody Crunch and his deputy ran up behind Ant. They pointed their weapons at the boys. 'Don't listen to this idiot,' Kody growled, nodding at the guard. 'He's in shock, he's talking rubbish.'

'But I heard you talking earlier,' said Ant. 'All the time you've been in the Parkworld "investigating", you had no intention of killing the rareio, did you, Kody Crunch? You were just studying it. And all because of this Operation Wipeout.'

Even though he could only see Kody's avatar, Ant saw the way he flinched when his name was spoken.

'So you know it's me?' said Kody.

'Oh yes,' replied Ant.

'Not such a nice guy after all, huh? You would have left my … the frozen gamers in hospital for years!' shouted Griff. He pointed his lightning rod at Kody but before he could use it, a strong beam flashed from the deputy's and knocked it from his hand.

'How much have you heard?' asked Kody.

'Enough,' said Ant.

Kody looked from one boy to the other, as though weighing up what kind of risk they posed. He walked up to Ant and laid the tip of his lightning rod on Ant's chest.

Pradahl responded immediately. She rose into the air, spreading her wings around him and baring her teeth in a warning snarl.

Kody and his deputy both turned their weapons on the dragon and fired. She was hit in the neck and chest and fell to the ground in a slack, lifeless heap.

'Pradahl!' cried Ant. He bent down. There was no movement, not a breath in her body. 'You've killed her!' he yelled. 'She wasn't attacking you, she was just trying to protect me!'

'Don't you understand yet?' The shadow of Kody Crunch fell across Ant as he cradled his dragon's head. 'This is all just a game, kid. It's not something to get worked up about. Even Operation Wipeout. It's just part of a game. Now let's discuss how we can solve this problem about what you think you heard.'

Ant placed Pradahl's head gently on the ground and looked up at Kody.

'What about the players in hospital? Was that part of your game?' he snapped.

He felt Griff's hand on his shoulder and heard Griff mutter 'Come on!' Ant's legs had turned to jelly but he managed to stand and walk away.

Kody came after them, his voice changing to the persuasive one he used in his adverts. How could he make this situation all right again? What did the boys want, maybe some vouchers for free games? How would they like to become testers for new Crunch Hut games that weren't even on the market yet? How would they like to star in his adverts and become famous? Think how jealous their friends would be!

'Let's get away,' said Griff. They began to run down the hill. Griff called out, 'Ready? One … two … three…'

At exactly the same moment, the two boys disappeared from the Parkworld. A split second later, they were back in the Dell.

Ant tore off his headset and flung it on the grass. 'They got her. They killed Pradahl. How dare Kody Crunch do that to my dragon? How dare he?'

His heart was hammering and he felt like screaming with frustration, but the investigators might hear him and put two and two together. Calm down, he told himself.

'I'm sorry, mate,' Griff laid his hand on Ant's shoulder. 'Do you think it could be – you know – temporary?'

'Nothing like that's ever happened in *Kismet*. I've never seen her die like that,' said Ant.

'Look, I'm going to have to ring my dad. You saw what happened in there, Kody and his deputy unfroze as soon as we destroyed the rareio.' Griff found his phone in his backpack and scrolled around the screen. 'I've got four missed calls from Dad!' he said excitedly. 'Ant, I'm so nervous. I have to call him right now and find out what's happening.'

This was the most important news and Ant tried to forget about Pradahl's lifeless body back in the Parkworld.

That was just a game, this was real life and real people's lives at stake. He waited, almost too scared to breathe as he watched Griff talk to his dad.

'Yeah? … Yeah? … She said what? What did the doctors say? … Yeah, sure Dad, I'll be home in twenty minutes and then we can head to the hospital to see her.'

When Griff rang off, he was crying tears of relief and he and Ant hugged each other. His mum had woken up!

Their celebration was cut short when they heard footsteps crunching through the undergrowth. They grabbed their stuff, realising that Kody and his team would be searching the area for the kids who had just destroyed the rareio. Only it wasn't Kody who stumbled out of the bushes but a really glum-looking girl.

'It's you, isn't it?' said the girl, eyeing Ant and Griff's suits. She was wearing an ordinary grey *Ray-Chay* suit and carrying a headset. 'You were in the Parkworld? I mean, if it *wasn't* you, then sorry, just ignore me. But it was, wasn't it? I've been right round the edge of the park searching. I didn't realise there were two of you.'

'Oh yes.' Ant took a breath. 'You must be the dolphin?'

She nodded. 'I'm Rubie Zhu Jenkins. I'm in the year above you at school. You're Ant. You're Griff, right? Our mums are friends, I think? So did the investigators ban you too?'

'Oh I know,' said Griff. 'Your mum owns the jewellery

shop in the high street, I've seen you in there. My mum spends hours in your shop while I'm sat outside in the car. Not that I'll ever complain again about anything my mum does.' He smiled at Ant, who smiled back and gave him a thumbs up.

'We'd better explain,' said Ant. 'We destroyed the rareio. My dragon got killed straight after.' He swallowed and looked at the floor, so Griff took over.

'My mum was one of the frozen gamers who's been in hospital. I just spoke to my dad on his phone and she's woken up. All the frozen gamers have.'

Rubie's mouth dropped open. 'I didn't realise your mum was one of them, that's awful … but now she's woken up, that's so wonderful! I'm so pleased for you.'

Someone called Rubie's name from the top of the path. Rubie yelled back in Chinese.

'It's my big brother,' she explained. 'I asked him to wait for me up there. He's not into any kind of gaming. He doesn't really know what I'm up to.'

'Back-up?' said Ant.

'Best I could do,' Rubie nodded. 'Listen, in the Parkworld, you asked if I'd heard what the investigators said, but I didn't stop to listen. I'm sorry. I guessed you were there for the same reason I was: to try and defeat the rareio. I wanted to beat you to it, so I jumped out first. Wish I hadn't now. So, what *did* the investigators say?'

'Bad stuff,' said Griff. 'You wouldn't want to know.'

'Yes, I would!' said Rubie. She looked annoyed. 'Look, I am a level 25 *Ray-Chay* player and I have just been banned permanently from a game I love. Please, tell me what those investigators said?'

Ant recognised something in Rubie. He knew what it was like to love a game and she'd been so brave in the Parkworld. He thought she probably did deserve an answer.

'First of all, the boss? That's Kody Crunch himself,' Ant began.

'No way!' said Rubie.

'Yeah, but don't get too impressed,' Griff chipped in. 'He's not the lovely guy we all thought. He's pure evil.'

Rubie shook her head in disbelief.

'It's not what we thought at all,' said Ant. 'Kody Crunch and his investigators were never there to kill the rareio. They didn't care whether the frozen gamers would wake up or not.'

'Especially Kody,' muttered Griff.

'But why?' said Rubie.

'We're not sure. There's something called Operation Wipeout. The guard was in shock and started telling us about it before Kody stepped in and stopped him. It looks like he's found some way of controlling people and it's got something to do with the rareio jumping into you.'

'But it went wrong this time,' said Griff. 'I guess it's because I corrupted the rareio. It became a rogue, didn't do what it was supposed to, and when it messed up the game, it messed up his precious Operation Wipeout too. You know, that kind of makes me feel better about the whole thing.'

'Hang on, hang on,' said Rubie incredulously. 'Kody's controlling people? Meaning he can make them do whatever he wants? You do mean … in the game?'

'Who knows?' said Ant. 'The frozen players were frozen in real life. There's so much we don't know about Operation Wipeout. You saw how much Kody wanted to buy our silence back there, offering us free games and stuff.'

The three of them stared at one another. The full force of what they'd discovered was only just dawning on them. Then they heard voices over in the park, angry voices coming closer.

'Hey, we'd better go,' said Rubie. 'I bet that's Kody and his crew. They won't like having two people out in the real world knowing all this.'

Ant, Rubie and Griff grabbed their belongings and ran up the path to the Parade.

17
THE CELESTIAL SEAMSTRESS

When Ant got home, he looked so fed up, Lia asked him if he'd had a row with someone at school or something. Then Lance came home from work, saying the investigators had announced they'd finally destroyed the rareio after an epic battle. The frozen gamers had woken up and everyone was congratulating Kody Crunch. No one was sure yet if *Ray-Chay* was still going to be playable. Apparently, he would be making some big announcement in the next few days.

Ant rolled his eyes when he heard Lance say Kody Crunch was a hero, but he didn't reveal what had really happened. Obviously, he was glad the frozen gamers were all right. He and Griff were the real ones responsible for waking them, and that made him feel proud. Yet the whole Operation Wipeout plan sounded so massive and evil, and he had absolutely no idea what to do about it. Ant had agreed to meet up with Griff and Rubie at lunchtime in school on Monday to talk more.

Although he knew it was a much smaller problem,

Ant was still churned up about Pradahl. For Kody Crunch to kill his dragon seemed like a very personal attack. It made Ant so angry to remember Pradahl's lifeless body on the ground. He'd always loved *Kismet Cosmos*, but he didn't feel like playing it any more. He couldn't bear playing without Pradahl. The thought of appearing on planet Zoberne without her was horrible and he couldn't face starting the whole game again with a new dragon. He wanted Pradahl, only Pradahl.

That evening Ant went to the table-tennis club, played a few games with some mates and felt better. When he got back home, he and Snoz shared a pizza and watched a funny movie. On Saturday, he and his dad went shopping in town for some new sports kit and had a brilliant day.

At last, on Sunday afternoon, Ant decided he was ready to face *Kismet Cosmos* again and make a final decision whether to save it or bin it. The Crunch Hut logo on the headset made him feel like hurling it against the wall, but he stopped himself.

So possibly for the last time, Ant put on the headset and haptic gloves. When he switched on the game, it took longer than usual for the volcano world to emerge. When it did, he was all alone. All the different planets he and Pradahl had travelled to, all the adventures they'd had together ... and now this. He'd always wondered what he'd do if *Kismet* came to an end, but now it could go on forever as far as he cared. Without his dragon by his side, he wasn't interested.

A light appeared in the sky and elongated into a familiar figure. The Celestial Seamstress always made a new suit of armour for his avatar Tarn each time Pradahl shed her scaly skin, just before they flew to a new planet.

'It is time for your new armour, Tarn,' she said in her tinkling voice, which always made him think of the Good Witch from *The Wizard of Oz*.

'No,' said Tarn. 'Pradahl is dead.' Ant could feel real tears pricking his eyes.

She didn't say anything. She floated in mid-air, smiling.

'Don't you get it? Pradahl is dead,' said Tarn. 'There's no new armour, no new planets. That's it.'

'Tarn,' said the Celestial Seamstress, 'there are many paths to take us to where we want to be.'

Was the Celestial Seamstress giving him some kind of hint?

He looked around. He was standing at the edge of a swamp with bushes on either side. A series of caves had been carved into the side of an extinct volcano. There were no paths to be seen.

Then something caught his eye, a small, black, intensely shiny object lying under a bush to his right. He walked over and picked it up. It was a coalberry. For a moment, Tarn tried to work out why this was so strange. Then he realised.

The bush wasn't a coalberry bush, but that wasn't it. There *were* no coalberry bushes on planet Zoberne. They only grew on the planet Aneome. He remembered cursing the fact that Pradahl had just one left in her inventory. What was a coalberry doing on this planet? Was it some kind of clue?

Tarn scanned the area for anything similar. A little way off, he found a small bottle of whistlejuice potion. With mounting excitement, Tarn remembered finding a bottle like this on planet Volare, and stashing it in Pradahl's inventory. He had never found a use for it: he had never needed Pradahl to emit an ear-piercing whistle.

A pulpa stone, a masterfang, wing extensions… Tarn carried on finding more and more items. They were leading him closer and closer to the caves. They were all items that could have been discarded from his dragon's inventory. But why?

Outside the smallest cave opening, Tarn saw what he thought was a puddle of lava. It was strange to find lava at the bottom of an extinct volcano. As he got nearer the puddle, he realised that it wasn't lava. It actually looked like … it actually *was*…

Tarn snatched up the fiery-red, scaly skin in wonder. He heard a small cough behind him. It was the Celestial

Seamstress. He passed the skin over to her and, as usual, in a whirlwind blink of an eye, she transformed it into a suit of armour which, after a couple of spins, he found himself wearing.

Tarn looked around excitedly. He knew what had always happened next in the game…

From the cave, Pradahl emerged, blinking in the sunlight and wearing a delicate golden coat, so young and tender the scales weren't even visible. As soon as she saw Tarn, she ran to him, blowing happy puffs of smoke, and butted him with her head. Tarn stroked her and hugged her, overjoyed.

He turned to the Celestial Seamstress, even though he could never normally talk with her like this. 'How is this possible? I saw her not breathing.'

She smiled. 'The lightning bolts left her in a state of shock, but that fiery skin and your dragon were both tougher than you realise. Retreating to *Kismet Cosmos* and the planet Zoberne, she used every last bit of strength to crawl to the cave to recover, her inventory of items falling from her as she went. She had shed her skin earlier than she would normally. You're going to have to take very good care of her.'

'I swear I'll look after you, Pradahl,' said Tarn. 'You really are the greatest dragon in the cosmos.'

'Before I go, I have a special gift for you,' said the

Celestial Seamstress. 'Pradahl could easily get hurt until her coat thickens up. You need this.' She held out her hand. In the palm lay a smouldering coal. 'It is a stealth ember. Keep this in Pradahl's inventory. If her life is in danger, activate it, but it can only be used once. This cannot, however, happen in *Kismet Cosmos.*'

This was really weird. The Celestial Seamstress seemed to know that Pradahl had left *Kismet.* But how could she know and why was she implying it could happen again?

'What does the stealth ember do?' asked Tarn. He thought he knew every item in *Kismet Cosmos,* but he had never heard of this one.

She gave a sad smile. 'There is only one. Only activate it in the most extreme circumstances. You have not yet reached the end of the game, so I cannot tell you more than that.'

Tarn thanked the Celestial Seamstress for this amazing, strange and almost scary gift. He watched it disappear from her hand with a shimmer. The shining scale on Pradahl's chest twinkled to show it had been stowed safely in her inventory.

'Now Tarn, you have not finished on Zoberne,' said the Celestial Seamstress. 'Or rather, the planet has not yet finished with you. Your time here is nearing an end, but there are still a few surprises left.'

Did she mean his time on the ninety-ninth planet, or in *Kismet Cosmos*? Ant didn't have the nerve to ask. Having Pradahl back made him realise how much he loved the game and hated the thought of coming to the end, even though that was bound to happen one day.

For now, it was enough to be with his dragon again.

18

THREE KIDS

On Monday, Ant and Rubie met at the tennis court at lunchtime. Griff was late. Ant went over everything he'd overheard Kody and his team talking about in the Parkworld. When Kody had freaked out at his guard, he'd said he stood to lose a load of money if his plan wasn't successful, but why would he even care that much, he was already a multi-millionaire? They both agreed that he was a greedy slimeball.

'A slimeball everyone's congratulating right now,' said Rubie and she started doing some weird but funny voices: '*Isn't he such an all-round great guy, saving all those people? Isn't he the smartest ever techie genius you ever met?*'

'And because Griff got the blame for the rareio going wrong in the first place, the creep looks completely blameless, even though it was his game they were playing when all those players got frozen.' Rubie was looking past Ant's shoulder as he said this and gave a slight shake of her head. Ant glanced behind and saw a suspiciously quiet group of kids watching them.

Without a word, he and Rubie turned and began walking up the field until they were sure they wouldn't be overheard. Ant took the cheese roll from his backpack and Rubie took a packet of sandwiches from hers. They began to eat as they walked along.

'We can't tell anyone, can we?' said Rubie, through a mouthful of tuna mayonnaise.

'I was about to say the same,' said Ant, shaking his head. 'People won't believe us if we say we killed the rareio. They'd think we were trying to get attention. And if we tell them what little we know about Operation Wipeout, they won't take us seriously.'

'Kody would just deny it anyway,' agreed Rubie. 'I mean, he's the owner of this massive games company and who are we? Three kids. By the way, where *is* the third kid?'

'Should be along soon,' said Ant.

A railway track ran parallel to the school field. Without warning, a train sped past and for two seconds Ant saw all the passengers squashed into their seats, each trusting the driver to take them where they wanted to go, to the destination written on their ticket. All of them so, so trusting, just like the gamers playing *Ray-Chay*.

'If only we could hire someone, like a detective, to go undercover and find out about Operation Wipeout,' said Ant. 'Get some real, hard evidence. Kody couldn't deny anything then, and everyone would find out what an Agrade slime he is. We could put a stop to it before anyone else gets hurt.'

'I suppose, in a way, we are undercover,' said Rubie. 'I mean, Kody doesn't know who we are. And if he is looking for you, he's only looking for two kids, isn't he? And there are three of us. That might be enough to throw him off the scent.'

It had already crossed Ant's mind that Kody might be looking for him and Griff. What would he do if he did track them down, try and bribe them again?

'At the moment, he doesn't have a clue who we are,' said Ant. 'You don't have to have an account to play *Ray-Chay*, everything's in the suit. Griff and I didn't use our real names in front of them. And our avatars don't look anything like us.'

They stood in silence and thought.

'I bet you any day now,' Ant started up again, 'Kody will make this big announcement, that *Ray-Chay's* one hundred percent safe and it's coming back, and before you know it, he'll be controlling people and getting them to do whatever he wants. How can we stop him?'

'I'd be too scared to play *Ray-Chay* again, even if I got another suit,' sighed Rubie. 'I think you're right. If the rareio can freeze those players in real life, Kody can probably control people in real life. What are we going to do?'

They spotted Griff running up the field towards them, weighed down by his heavy backpack. Panting heavily when he got to them, he dumped the backpack on the ground and bent forwards, holding his knees, as he tried to get his breath back.

'Griff, mate, where were you?' said Ant.

'Maths,' he said. 'Half the class … hadn't done their homework … Mr Lloyd gave everyone an ear-bashing.'

'That is so unfair,' said Rubie. 'If you're in the half that has done their homework and you've got to sit there for ages being lectured like that.'

'What? Oh, yeah…' Griff gave a sheepish little smile. 'It is really annoying, you're right.'

Rubie raised her eyebrows and Ant smirked at her. Rubie's half of the class clearly wasn't Griff's half.

'How's your mum?' asked Ant.

'Same as ever,' Griff chuckled even though he was still panting. 'Soon as she got home, she was finding things to moan about. She had a go at me for not tidying my room! It's fantastic to have her back, though. I apologised to her for taking the rareio and I've promised to do loads of jobs around the house to try to make up for it. Listen, guys, I have got to tell you something and you're not going to believe it…'

He stood up straight and Ant saw that he was bursting with news, his eyes like saucers.

'All this time, Kody Crunch has been staying at my parents' hotel and I never knew!'

Ant and Rubie's jaws dropped. There were just no words.

Griff carried on. 'They've all been there. They've been eating in their rooms and using the back entrance to come and go. Most of them have left now, except Kody and a couple of others. Only my Dad and a handful of the staff knew. Kody swore them to secrecy in case the press camped out on the lawns, trying to get an interview with him. Dad was happy to co-operate because he thought Kody was doing his best to help Mum.' Griff's face clouded over at this last bit.

'Oh man, that's rough,' said Ant.

Griff visibly swallowed his anger and carried on. 'Dad's only told me now because they think it's all over. Apparently, *Ray-Chay* is coming back and Kody's going to hold a press conference at the hotel tomorrow to reassure everybody that it's super-safe. Straight after that, he's leaving.'

'We've got to do something!' said Rubie.

'This could be our last chance to find out about Operation Wipeout,' agreed Ant. 'Griff, mate, this is incredible! Is there any way you can sneak us in there?'

'Come with me after school,' said Griff. 'There might be some way of getting close to Kody. We could listen in on what he's saying.'

'Like detectives.' Rubie nodded at Ant. 'If we could only get close enough, I could use my phone to record him. That would be hard evidence we could take to the newspapers or the police. Kody Crunch would be exposed for what he is.'

All three stared at one another with mounting excitement.

Ant noticed the lower end of the field was beginning to clear, a sign that the bell was about to ring. Griff fumbled in his backpack for his sandwiches and ate hurriedly as they walked back to the school building.

'I don't think I ever said thanks,' he said to Ant. 'For helping get Mum back, mate. I'm sorry I behaved like such an idiot, you know, before it all happened.'

He stopped and did a very old-fashioned thing: stuck out his hand for Ant to shake. The fact he had half a sandwich hanging out of his mouth at the time didn't spoil the moment.

'That's okay,' said Ant, thinking it was amazing how people could change.

'I'm sorry for a lot of things,' said Griff. 'Including getting so obsessed with *Ray-Chay* in the first place.'

'Like my dad says: You've got to be bigger than the game,' said Ant.

'But are you all right, Ant,' Rubie asked, 'after your dragon from that other game got destroyed?'

'Pradahl?' said Ant. 'Well, I've got a bit of good news there too...' And he told them all about it as they walked back into school.

19

DETECTIVE WORK

The Oak Suite, on the first floor, was the fanciest suite in the King's Elm Hotel-plus-Health-Spa. It was where honeymoon couples usually stayed, with an emperor-size four-poster bed, a whirlpool bath and a balcony overlooking a small lake, where they could eat breakfast while admiring the swans. To a multi-millionaire like Kody Crunch, the Oak Suite was probably slumming it. Nevertheless this is where he'd been living since his secret arrival in Westford Abbey. Griff's dad had told him Kody had rented the whole floor. The other bedrooms were for his investigators or just kept empty, as Kody hadn't wanted any members of the public staying there and spotting him. Most of his team had left now, as would Kody after the press conference.

The cleaning cupboard right next to the Oak Suite wasn't nearly as glamorous, but this is where Ant and Rubie hid after school with Griff, who had sneaked the key from the main desk downstairs. There wasn't much room, with a vacuum cleaner in there and the trolley the cleaners used, piled high with clean towels, soaps, tea bags and individually wrapped biscuits. Clean bedding was stored on shelves on one side of the cupboard, but the wall adjoining the Oak Suite was empty and right now the three kids had their ears stuck to that wall, trying to listen to the conversation on the other side.

'Hang on,' whispered Rubie. 'We're doing this wrong. There's a trick I remember from old detective films.' She took a drinking glass from the trolley, the sort that held the guests' toothbrushes. She held the bottom of the glass to her ear while pressing the open end to the wall. She beamed a huge grin and gave them a thumbs up, so Ant and Griff copied her.

Suddenly it was much easier to hear what was being said and they could even make out who was speaking. In a weird echo of the Parkworld, Ant recognised not only Kody Crunch's voice but also his deputy and the guard's voices.

'I can't wait to get out of here,' said Kody. They could hear him pacing from one end of the room to the other.

'One more day,' said his deputy. 'Soon as the press conference is over tomorrow, we can get going. None of us will ever have to set foot in crummy Westford Abbey again.'

'Can't wait,' agreed the guard.

'You did real good, Kody,' the deputy said. 'Heck, you did great. *Ray-Chay* will come back more popular than ever, I know it.'

'And just because you didn't find out what went wrong with that rareio...' added the guard.

'Just button it, Norm!' Kody rounded on him. 'Thank you, Cheryl, that's sweet of you to say so.'

In the cupboard, Ant, Rubie and Griff glanced at one another. Now they knew the deputy was 'Cheryl' and the guard was 'Norm'. Their relationships sounded pretty similar to the Parkworld, with Norm getting picked on by Kody, even though he seemed to be the only one saying anything sensible. If Ant hadn't felt so anti everyone to do with Crunch Hut, he might have felt sorry for Norm.

Kody was clearly in a bad mood. 'If I could only lay hands on those stupid kids,' he growled. 'Showing up like that and spoiling everything.'

'Perhaps we should put some warning out with the *Ray-Chay* suit. Something like: "Each player must only wear their suit with the correct headset"? It might stop little idiots like the Lansdowne boy stealing a higher-level player's headset to wear with his own suit.'

Inside the cupboard, Griff made a face at the wall.

'It's an idea, Cheryl. We can't let anything like this happen again. No one would want to play it anymore, and when I think of all the money I've spent developing Operation Wipeout...'

Ant, Rubie and Griff gave each other meaningful looks. This was Kody's first mention of Operation

Wipeout. Rubie took her mobile phone from her pocket, scrolled about to find the 'record' button and held the phone to the bottom of the glass. Ant and Griff carried on listening.

'They'll be queuing up to pay me for playing Wipeout, all the big guys who need some schmucks to do their dirty work for them. How's that for a great game, controlling people, getting them to do whatever the highest bidder wants, while pocketing all the money? Brilliant!'

So it was true: Operation Wipeout was about controlling players in real life. Gamers would be brainwashed to do whatever Kody Crunch wanted, and Kody was willing to sell the service to anyone willing to pay for it. It didn't bear thinking about, what horrible tasks these gamers might be made to perform.

'They'll be here before long with the meal,' said Cheryl. 'I ordered lobster tonight, Kody, I hope that's okay? We could eat on the dinky little balcony out there and watch the swans again.'

'Sure, sounds amazing,' said Kody sarcastically. 'Another lobster and swans evening. Whoopie-doo. Anyway, straight after that treat, I'm going back into *Ray-Chay.* There are still a few empty avatar plugs to clear out of my cache. And there's nothing to stop me making a new rareio. Or a whole batch of them. Why not?'

'You want us in there too, boss?' asked Norm.

'Sure, getting rid of the avatar plugs is kind of slow work, there'll be plenty for you to help me with,' replied Kody. 'I'll set up an unsecure connection, so you can enter my world again.'

'Oh Kody, that'd be just great,' gushed Cheryl. 'It's such a blast visiting your *Ray-Chay* world. It's so beautiful there.'

'Just don't mess up, right, Norm? Don't press anything or do anything unless I tell you.'

There was a knock on the Oak Suite door and Ant heard the waiter wheel in the trolley, presumably carrying the finest lobster and champagne. He heard the huge French door onto the balcony slide open and the voices left the room. It was impossible to hear anything now and Ant signalled to Rubie to finish recording.

As soon as they were sure the waiter had gone back to the kitchen, Ant signalled to the others to follow him. They left the cupboard, tiptoed down the corridor and left the building via the fire escape.

At the bottom of the fire escape was a shady, neglected strip of garden. Ant, Rubie and Griff stopped there and began to whisper, all at once. *So it was true, Operation Wipeout was as evil as they'd suspected... What on earth was he going to brainwash the gamers to do?... Now Kody was planning on making more rareios, perhaps a whole army of them!*

Griff was still massively miffed at being referred to as a 'little idiot'.

'Oh, hang on,' said Rubie. 'Let's see if we've got that hard evidence.'

She scrolled about on her phone until she found the recording and pressed play. Ant and Griff crowded round and the three of them strained to make out a single word, but the voices sounded no louder than a buzzing bluebottle.

'Couldn't the recording be enhanced in a lab?' asked Griff. 'I'd really love to get those guys after everything they've done.'

Rubie shrugged her shoulders. Her recording didn't prove anything.

'You know, it was so weird the way he was talking back there,' said Ant. 'He said he had to clear his cache out before making more rareios, as if his *Ray-Chay* world is some kind of command centre.'

'He's a thrill-seeker,' said Rubie. 'I can't imagine him sitting at some desk and controlling these players. It's more fun to be actually inside the game.'

'He's a flipping thrill-seeking maniac,' agreed Griff. 'But the worst of it is, all these gamers are putting their lives in his hands.'

Kody Crunch had to be stopped, and time was ticking by. The next day he would be leaving for home.

'Look,' said Ant. 'You two wait here, I'm going to sprint home and get my *Ray-Chay* suit and my *Kismet* headset. I can put them on, like I did before, and hide in the cleaning cupboard. If it really is an unsecure connection, I should be able to get into Kody Crunch's world too.'

The other two made faces, as if they weren't sure about the idea. 'Okay,' said Griff slowly, 'but what do you plan on doing when you're in there?'

'I don't know yet,' said Ant. 'I will have Pradahl to protect me and she's got that stealth ember in her inventory, although I've got no idea what it does. She and I can do a bit of detective work, find out what those "avatar plugs" are for a start. The more information we've got, the more we could eventually take to the police. At the moment, our evidence is practically nil and they wouldn't take us seriously.'

'We can stand guard outside in the corridor,' said Rubie. 'And warn you if there's any danger.'

'Perfect,' said Ant. 'Okay, I'm going to run home. I'll be back as soon as I can.'

20
KODY'S CACHE

Ant was so out of breath when he returned, he had to wait a couple of minutes before climbing the fire escape to the first floor. Griff and Rubie were waiting to let him in. Rubie was dressed in one of the cleaners' aprons, with a large yellow duster sticking out of the front pocket. There was no point in Griff disguising himself. The Crunch Hut guys all knew him as the owners' son, so it wouldn't seem suspicious for him to be hanging about.

They had moved the trolley into the corridor to give Ant more space to move around. The last thing they needed were any suspicious bumps and thumps coming from the cleaning cupboard. It also gave Rubie a great cover for standing there on guard. She could re-fold the towels and sort out a load of mixed up tea bags, soaps and biscuits, arranging everything neatly on the trolley. Griff would keep guard on the stairs further down the corridor.

While Ant had been gone, Rubie and Griff had invented some secret signals. One meant 'Someone's coming up the stairs,' another meant 'someone's leaving

Kody's bedroom' and a third meant 'Get Ant out of the cupboard now!' They really hoped the third signal wouldn't be needed.

Inside the cupboard, Ant got dressed in the *Ray-Chay* suit as quickly as he could. He could hear voices in the room and it sounded as though Kody and Co were already in his *Ray-Chay* world. Ant put on his *Kismet* headset and flicked the switch. It took a little while before he found himself and Pradahl in the game.

He'd been dreading these first few moments because there was no way of knowing where he would find himself and who would be there. To his relief, he and Pradahl found themselves all alone in a garden. They hid in the shade of a huge cedar tree. A white mansion stood nearby. Ant recognised it, having seen it so many times in Crunch Hut adverts. It was a copy of Kody Crunch's real-life mansion, the place which obviously meant the most to him. This version seemed exaggerated, with bigger pillars and taller towers. A fleet of mirror-shiny sports cars were parked in front of the house and beside them stood a massive golden statue of Kody which had never been in the ads. The statue Kody was flashing his finger pistols straight at him and this made Ant nervous.

Ant had appeared in the game as Tarn, although he didn't think of himself as Tarn anywhere but *Kismet Cosmos.* Kody would instantly recognise his avatar from the Parkworld if he saw him. Pradahl looked different, of course, with her golden coat. Ant was worried by the sight of her delicate skin and he pressed the shining scale in her chest to bring up her inventory. There was the smouldering stealth ember, but he would obey the Seamstress and only use it if her life was being threatened. It had to be some amazing item for this to be the only one in existence. Ant wished he knew more.

'Come on, Pradahl,' Ant whispered and together they crept around the edge of the lawn, sticking to the shadows. There was a huge conservatory at the side of the house holding a forest of palm trees, a small waterfall and a rainbow-coloured collection of butterflies, fish, frogs and lizards. Hearing no one, Ant led the way in.

The house was all decorated with so much bling, it hurt the eyes. There were big selfie pictures of Kody Crunch on every wall and Ant could imagine that when Kody wasn't admiring these, he was catching sight of his own reflection in the mirrored ceiling and the vast array of mirrored tables and ornaments, including a mirrored chandelier the size of a small car.

Kody certainly loves himself, thought Ant.

They heard voices and just had time to hide themselves behind a copy of the famous statue called *The Thinker*, which showed a man sitting deep in thought with his head resting on his hand. Of course, in this version the man was Kody Crunch, sunglasses and all. Cheryl and Norm walked in carrying big boxes, which they placed on the ground a couple of metres from Ant and Pradahl's hiding place.

'What does he want us to do with these?' Norm sounded tired.

Cheryl did too. 'Outside, I think. He'll show us in a moment.'

Ant craned his neck as much as he dared to peer into one of the boxes. It contained large electrical plugs, each with a picture of a different avatar on the back.

Norm threw himself down on a black leather sofa.

'Get up, he'll see you!' hissed Cheryl. 'You know he doesn't like us lounging about.'

'I can't help it. I'm exhausted,' said Norm. 'Isn't there an easier way of doing this? It's a game and he's a coding genius. Can't he just magic up a bit of code to make these avatar plugs disappear back to the … wherever.'

'If only,' said Cheryl. 'He tried, but the corrupted rareio messed that up. The only way Kody's found to disengage the avatar plugs is literally tugging them out of the sockets.'

'It's like pulling out walrus teeth,' said Norm. 'And how many are left? Seven? Eight?'

'Nine. And he wants them all out today.' Cheryl was definitely not her usual sparkly self.

Even though he was exhausted, Norm sprang to his feet as soon as Kody Crunch appeared, carrying an identical box. 'Hope you're not slacking, Norm,' warned Kody. 'Okay, we'll dump these down the garden. Once they start playing again, their avatar plugs will disappear, but I don't want them cluttering up my mansion. It just reminds me of ... what happened.'

Ant wiggled his eyebrows at Pradahl and she butted him ever so gently. He was pleased that Kody was still upset about his precious rareio.

'When they're all out, you can clean up my cache while I set about making new rareios in the lab,' Kody continued.

'Boss, seriously, can't we just leave the game for twenty minutes and have a rest in the real world? I'm thirsty,' said Norm.

Kody sighed. 'You too, Cheryl?' he asked. Cheryl must have nodded because then he said, 'We'll get rid of these, then we'll go get a drink. But when you get back, you'll have to work twice as hard. I just want to forget this whole horrible episode and move on.'

The three of them picked up their boxes and headed out via the conservatory. Ant signalled for Pradahl to follow him further into the house. This was their best chance to find Kody's cache, then leave before he returned.

Ant had a new idea. What if they wrote down everything they knew about Operation Wipeout and included details of Kody's cache that you could only know if you'd been in there? What if they sent it to the local newspaper anonymously? If a journalist asked an awkward question at the press conference the next day, how would Kody react? If he blew his top with the whole world watching, wouldn't people start getting suspicious?

The mansion was like a rabbit warren, but the décor was the same: selfies and bling. Even Kody Crunch's mum might have found it a bit much. Pradahl padded after him for a while, but then her curiosity must have got the better of her. Ant glanced behind and she wasn't there. He went to find her.

She'd strayed into what was obviously Kody's lab. There were rows and rows of coloured chemicals in bottles and the most amazing equipment: glass cauldrons, curly pipes, and funnels the size of a French horn. Was this where Kody created new rareios? Were the 'chemicals' actually bits of code he mixed together, only he liked playing at being Doctor Frankenstein while he did it? Ant would like to have poked about for a bit longer but there was no time. He wanted to find the cache. He was sure nothing would wind Kody up as much as thinking some unknown player had been inside his command centre.

The low-lit purple corridor began to lead round and round with no rooms on either side, and Ant felt like a tiny silver ball being rolled around a maze in one of those games that come out of a cracker. The circle got tighter and tighter until right in the middle they came to an escalator. Ant and Pradahl travelled upwards to an enormous round room, with no windows but with a glass floor showing all the rooms below. The ceilings of those rooms must all be two-way mirrors. Maybe Kody was paranoid about intruders in his *Ray-Chay* world. Ant realised just how lucky they'd been not to have been spotted earlier.

He turned his attention to the rest of the room. Half the wall was made up of sliding panels, like black petals on a daisy. One had been pulled out. It held twenty-nine three-pin sockets coloured and shaped like the peppermint-flavour rareio. Nine of the avatar plugs were still in place, including that of Lady Cora. Twenty-nine — like the twenty-nine players who'd been frozen. In Kody's world they had literally been plugged into that rareio! Ant shuddered. It seemed as though Kody only needed to remove these remaining nine plugs before he could begin Operation Wipeout again.

Ant went snooping around the large semicircular control desk with its lights and dials and switches. He counted ten large screens on the other half of the wall, probably the way Kody intended watching the players as he controlled them.

Before long, Ant felt he had seen as much as he

needed to see. It was time to leave. He reached behind his head to switch off his *Kismet* headset.

'Not so fast,' came a voice.

21
THE STEALTH EMBER

'Did you really think I hadn't spotted you earlier?' chuckled Kody. He was pointing one lightning rod at Ant and another at Pradahl, who immediately grew out her wings and rose into the air, preparing to produce a fireball.

'Pradahl, no!' yelled Ant. She looked at Ant uncertainly and remained hovering.

'I think it's wise not to,' said Kody. 'That skin looks very young and new. It would only take one blast to finish her off completely. This new coat on her only confirms what I'd suspected: she's a *Kismet Cosmos* dragon, right?'

Reluctantly, Ant nodded.

For a moment, it didn't look like Kody would stop laughing. 'That stupid old game?' he said. 'You must be the last player on Earth!'

'But it is the earliest Crunch Hut game?' said Ant. Why would Kody keep putting down his own game like this? It didn't make sense.

'Yes, well, it shouldn't have been,' Kody frowned. 'I was hoping everyone had forgotten about it.'

Keeping one eye on Ant, he began drawing bars of a cage around Pradahl while she floated in the air. Pradahl gave one sideways zap, but Kody replied with a lightning bolt aimed just above her head.

'Keep still, Pradahl,' ordered Ant. He knew Kody was right. With her skin so young and tender, one blast would kill her outright. If only he could activate the stealth ember. Surely this was the ideal moment to use it?

'So what do you think of this place?' asked Kody, as he continued to cage in Pradahl.

'Very impressive,' said Ant.

'I suppose you've guessed that right now in real life, my agents are searching the hotel for the player who's managed to infiltrate my game for the second time?'

Ant hadn't guessed, and it took a lot to keep his voice steady. He prayed that Rubie and Griff were doing a good job of misdirecting them. He didn't want to be stopped from playing. He was sure that in the small lag after he switched off the headset, Kody would kill Pradahl.

'Cheryl and Norm are searching for me?' said Ant. 'Well, good luck with that.'

Kody half smiled. 'Well, Norm isn't the sharpest tool in the box. You know what I could do with? A really smart kid like you to come and join my team. Someone young and quick. Someone who reminds me of me when I was your age.'

Ant could have said something insulting, but he didn't. He listened as Kody carried on.

'When I get Operation Wipeout working – because I am going to, one way or another – I will probably end up being the richest guy in the world. Come and work for me and you'll be super-rich beyond your wildest dreams. In an annoying way, you impressed me in the Parkworld and you've impressed me here too. The beauty of it is, we wouldn't even need to meet … Tarn.' Kody read out the name floating beside Ant's avatar in ghostly letters. 'We'd only have to meet here, in my virtual world. You'd be the only other player with a key.'

Ant looked up at Pradahl, who was now completely caged. She huffed out a miserable wisp of smoke.

'Say yes and I'll call off Cheryl and Norm,' Kody continued, in his weaselly advert voice. 'Say yes and you can have your pet dragon back. Come on, Tarn. It's really not that bad being a bad guy. You get to have loads of stuff!' He gestured round at the command centre.

Ant could have cried. He wanted to say 'no' but what would happen then? All he could do was keep Kody talking.

'I just wish *Ray-Chay* was more like *Kismet Cosmos*,' he said, changing the subject. 'I don't care if nobody else plays any more. It's the best game I've ever come across.'

Kody's face fell. 'You have got to be kidding me,' he

said. '*Kismet Cosmos* was the old days. I always hated it. There are so many flaws in that terrible game. It's because I didn't actually work on it. For a smart kid, you have shocking taste.'

'You're wrong, *Kismet* is amazing,' Ant protested. It suddenly felt like he was having an argument with a mate in the school playground over whose game was best. 'To start with, the items in *Kismet* are so much stronger than anything in *Ray-Chay*. It's much more exciting to play.'

Out in the real world, Ant could hear banging. Someone was knocking on the door of the cleaner's cupboard. He would have to hurry up.

He'd just learned that Kody hadn't coded *Kismet Cosmos* himself. Would he even know what a stealth ember was?

'Press her shining scale now,' said Ant. 'You'll see how great the items are. There's a glowing rock in there, if you activate it, it'll give Pradahl super-strength to break the bars of that pathetic cage.'

'Oh yeah?' Kody was getting riled. 'These bars are impregnable. If you think your piddly rock can help her get out, I pity you!'

'Prove it then,' said Ant.

'Okay I will!' said Kody.

He reached with the end of the lightning rod and pressed Pradahl's shining scale. Up came her inventory. It was easy to see the item Ant meant. It was the least colourful of the lot.

'That thing? I'll show you...' said Kody and he activated the stealth ember.

Pradahl's skin began to crackle with black fuzz. Kody stepped back.

'What's that?' he shouted, but there wasn't time to say much else because the bars of the cage were melting onto the floor. Anything the melting bars touched melted too. In moments, there were gaping holes in the floor.

Kody watched in horror as the effect spread around the downstairs rooms, decimating his selfies and bling. Pradahl flew around the room, and the black fuzz dropped in heaps on the desk and splattered up the screens. Everything it touched melted. Ant's last view of Kody was of him plunging through one of these holes in the floor and disappearing down a tunnel, down, down into the melting heart of his *Ray-Chay* world.

Swooping past, Pradahl just rescued Ant before he did the same. The stealth ember's effect on Pradahl had now worn off. Ant decided to get out of the game at once.

Back in the cupboard, Rubie was shaking his arm. A loud, shrieking alarm was going off in the building. 'Didn't you hear me knocking on the door?' she asked. 'Get out of your suit quickly, that's the fire alarm.'

'Is there time?' asked Ant. 'If there's a fire we should just run out.'

'There's no fire,' Rubie assured him. 'It's Griff's way of getting Kody and the others out of the building. Everyone's being evacuated. Come on, it'll look strange if we're still in here.'

Ant changed quickly while Rubie took off her apron. She peered outside before signalling to Ant to follow her out. The cleaning trolley was still by the door, piled high with towels. Ant and Rubie joined Griff by the fire escape at the end of the corridor and the three of them went down the stairs. Once outside, they hid behind a bush and watched everyone else gathering on the front lawn.

'Look, there they are!' said Griff.

Kody, Cheryl and Norm were arguing on the far side of the lawn. Kody was pointing up at the first floor then burying his head in his hands and walking in circles.

'What on earth happened in *Ray-Chay*?' asked Rubie.

Ant told them about how he'd got Kody to activate the stealth ember and the three of them had to hold their hands over their mouths to stop themselves laughing out loud. Then Griff filled Ant in on how he'd kept Cheryl and Norm away from the cupboard for as long as he could, unlocking all the empty bedrooms for them. The whole story was hilarious.

'Do you think *Ray-Chay*'s destroyed?' asked Griff.

'I don't know,' said Ant. 'The stealth ember won't have done it much good.'

'But Pradahl's okay?' asked Rubie.

'Yes,' said Ant with a relieved smile.

Griff's dad emerged from the front entrance and waved his hands, asking for the guests' attention. 'It looks like it's a false alarm, folks. We apologise but we're sure you understand, there's nothing more important than the safety of our guests. Please will you wait here for about twenty minutes while we conduct a thorough search?'

Kody went rushing up to Griff's dad, ranting and raving like a spoilt child. They watched Griff's dad shake his head firmly before disappearing back into the hotel.

'It'll do him good for someone to say no to him for once,' sniggered Griff and yet again Ant noticed how much his friend had changed. 'Anyway, my dad won't mind that the fire alarm went off. They have to have practices from time to time. I'll own up and say I bumped into it by accident.'

'That press conference tomorrow is going to be really interesting,' said Rubie.

Ant told them about his earlier idea of getting a journalist to ask a question. They all agreed that after the stealth ember, it would be better to just watch what happened.

'We might have stopped Kody this time,' said Ant. 'But

from what he said to me, he's determined to get Operation Wipeout working, if not in *Ray-Chay* then in some other game.'

He paused, working up the nerve to tell them his idea. Would they think it was stupid?

'I've been thinking. Why don't we start a proper detective agency? The cover story would be, we'd be helping out players with problems in games, like if they'd got super-stuck on a level, for example, and finding out what was wrong. We could call ourselves "Games Detectives". It'd pay us a bit of pocket money and we could do it round my sister's flat on weekends.'

'Yeah,' said Griff, jumping about. 'We could get advertising cards made and hand them out round school. They could say something like:

Something weird in your game?
Something you just can't explain?
Don't give up cos it's a pain –
Call the Games Detectives!'

'That's amazing!' said Rubie. 'But that's just the cover story?'

'Yes,' said Ant. 'It would mean we'd get to hear about odd things in games, especially Crunch Hut ones. If something weird happens in someone's game, like a hint of a rareio, we get in and look for clues. It'd be one way of keeping tabs on what Kody Crunch is up to.'

They all smiled. It felt good to have a plan.

Ant, Rubie and Griff stayed watching Kody and the others arguing until everyone was told they could go back into the hotel.

22
KISMET HEAVEN

The next day, Griff and Rubie came to Ant's flat at teatime and they watched that morning's Crunch Hut press conference online. Kody sat on his own behind the long table, looking really glum, while tech journalists from all over the world asked him questions. The huge announcement was *Ray-Chay* would not be coming back. Not ever. An especially destructive virus had spread from the game to the server and all the game files had been lost. Ant swallowed. So the stealth ember had actually been a virus? Wasn't that a strange item for a game?

Kody went on to say that of course, this would be a massive blow to all *Ray-Chay* players around the world. He promised not only to buy back all the suits but to give every player a voucher to spend on the next new Crunch Hut game, which would be even better. 'It's the least I can do,' they watched him say, through gritted teeth.

The three kids jumped around, laughing and celebrating wildly. When Lance walked in, he wondered what was happening.

'Haven't you lot heard about *Ray-Chay*?' he said.

'Errr ... yes!' said Ant. 'Just now.'

'Well, we're in for a busy time at the shop.' Lance whistled through his teeth. 'Think of all those suits being returned. It's going to cost Kody Crunch a pretty penny, I can tell you.'

'He's just got to be bigger than the game,' said Ant.

Again, Lance wondered why the three of them fell about laughing.

It was time to return to *Kismet Cosmos.*

Tarn was finally coming to the end of his time on Zoberne, the ninety-ninth planet. He had located all the keys by following the puzzle paths and defeating the rotgoblins. He had unlocked the lava mantle chest with the rubyate key and the oceanic mantle chest with the sapphira key, and only had the earth mantle chest left to find. Once he found it, he would be able to open it with the emarala key which was tucked into the girdle of his dragonskin armour.

Pradahl's golden coat was now tough enough for Tarn to be able to ride on her back. He clung to his dragon as she swooped around the violent, violet skies. Tarn was going to miss this strange prehistoric planet with its belching volcanos and tidal swamps. It wasn't the prettiest in the cosmos but it was where he'd found Pradahl again and he'd never forget it.

Far below, nordeaters scuffled in the mud, creating swirling mazes and making strange crying sounds when they got stuck up dead ends. Lava flowers exploded on the sides of the volcanos like cannons firing pollen bombs. Lumogrubs flitted here and there with tiny torches rotating on their backs like mini-lighthouses.

Tarn spotted the earth mantle chest. It was sitting in the shade of a hundred-eye tree. All the eyes focused upon Pradahl and followed her course as she glided to the ground, her wings outspread.

Tarn fitted the emarala key into the lock and turned it. The lid sprang open and out popped a flagon of health. With the flagons of strength and wisdom from the other two chests, this would be enough to fuel their flight to the next planet: level up, in other words. Pradahl didn't need to shed her skin because she already had.

Tarn and Pradahl drank from the three flagons. This was always a part of the game Tarn looked forward to most, because you never knew what surprises the next planet might hold. He climbed on to Pradahl's back and held on to the ridged scales on her shoulders. Pradahl rose on her hind legs and her wings grew bigger and wider as she prepared for take-off.

Something stopped her. Pradahl's wings dropped to the floor. Both she and Tarn could feel something unusual.

The whole planet was rotating faster and faster. Ant

was worried – was this the end of *Kismet Cosmos?* Was he about to discover what waited at the end of the universe? He didn't want this to be the end.

But surely the ninety-ninth planet was a weird place to finish? Couldn't he have just one planet more? Planet 100, please?

Tarn clung on to Pradahl as Zoberne went whizzing round like a drunken carousel. The rushing wind was deafening. Lava spilling from the volcanos seemed to be forming shaky words in the sky. It was like watching the world's worst cake decorator at work. No, they really were words, he could read them.

Check the port ... check the port...

What port? What port?

Pradahl was battling to remain on her feet. She crouched low and used her wings like crutches to steady herself against the battering wind.

'Pradahl, I'm going to check something on the headset. I'll be back soon,' shouted Tarn above the din.

Ant didn't turn off the game but removed the headset and inspected it. He could still hear the tinny sound of wind inside. There was a small square port at the back of the headset which Ant had never used. He'd never known what it was for. Now it was glowing red. Nothing else seemed different about the headset and nothing was obviously wrong. Nervously, Ant put it back on.

The spinning had stopped. He was alone, but then Pradahl came racing to meet him, excited. They weren't on planet Zoberne anymore. They appeared to be up in the clouds, standing knee-deep in mist with nothing to see except the clear blue sky above and a magical hint of stars and planets beyond. 'So this is what happens at the end,' thought Ant. 'Kismet Heaven.'

Tarn took a few steps around the flat, featureless landscape. Is this where he and Pradahl were meant to live now, as some kind of reward? Were there adventures in heaven? Tarn returned to Pradahl and stroked her nose. In return, she butted his shoulder gently with her forehead, then looked at him as if asking what to do next. Tarn shrugged his shoulders. Was this it?

Ant was just getting to the point of leaving the game, because he couldn't stand such an anti-climax, when one star ahead brightened, then elongated into the familiar figure of the Celestial Seamstress.

'No more new suits of armour, Tarn.' Her voice rang out like a bell. 'No more new coats for you, Pradahl. You have proved yourself the greatest dragon in the cosmos.'

This was great news on the one hand, but disappointing on the other. Tarn was bored with this place already. Couldn't he just send himself back to one of his favourite planets to play again?

'So that's it?' said Tarn. 'No more *Kismet Cosmos*?'

She smiled and the faraway stars began to brighten and sing, an ever-rising chorus of *aahhs*. Something was happening.

'You can call me Celeste.' She winked.

'I don't understand … Celeste.'

'You are the only player in history to reach the end of *Kismet Cosmos*,' said Celeste. 'And your reward is simple and forever. Tarn, from now on, you can take your dragon into any game.'

It took him a moment to understand what she meant. Then he got it. The port! It was a way of connecting *Kismet Cosmos* up with other gaming machines!

'Do you mean just Crunch Hut games? Ones built with the same game engine?'

Celeste seemed to know exactly what Tarn would ask next, they were so in tune with one another. 'I mean any game, any at all. From now on, Pradahl will be able to help you in a thousand different worlds. Your adventures together will never have to end.'

'This is amazing,' said Tarn. It was slowly sinking in. 'But I don't understand how it's possible.'

'You're the first player to complete *Kismet Cosmos*. You have proved yourself and now you can take your skills and your dragon and play in any game. I would have also given you the stealth ember at this point, but I can see it has already been used.'

Celeste stopped. With one final smile, she shrank and turned back into a star. In a weird way, this looked like some kind of invitation. Tarn pulled out his broadsword and moved the tip around the sky, like a cursor. When it rested on Celeste's star, he clicked on it and a voice, clear as a bell, sang out the purest note. Tarn clicked on other stars. Each sang out in a different note. Why was this? Why would this feature have been programmed into the game unless it did something?

Ant decided to stop thinking of Tarn and play as himself. Celeste didn't come back when he clicked on the stars so Ant tried to remember what she'd said. Perhaps she'd given him some kind of clue. Nothing Ant could remember seemed to shine any light on this.

Light. Light? Ant looked at the twinkling stars and wondered. He dredged his memory for songs about stars. One kept coming to mind, the most famous. It was a song he hadn't sung since he was little, but still one of the most famous songs in the world. The 'How I wonder what you are?' line fitted how he was feeling. Ant set to work and managed to click on the stars to put all the notes of 'Twinkle Twinkle Little Star' in the right order.

As soon as Ant played the final note of the second line, he hit the jackpot. A small screen opened amongst the clouds and a real girl's face appeared. She did look a bit like Celeste, except she had short brown hair and wore glasses. She also looked like someone Ant had seen in adverts many times. Although the girl smiled, she didn't speak with much enthusiasm.

'Hey, you found me.' She gave a small wave. 'I wondered if anyone ever would. I hoped somebody would, because if you have, you are one superstar player and to be frank, the world may well need you. I'm Kelly Crunch. Or "Celeste", if you like. I'm the main designer and builder of *Kismet Cosmos*. It's my game. And it's all been about finding you.' She pointed at Ant and, for a moment, it looked a lot like Kody pointing his finger pistols.

'My brother and I began Crunch Hut together but we keep arguing. He's so annoyed I brought *Kismet* out as our first game, when some game he was working on failed. Anyway, now I've decided to leave. He's got ambitions for this company I don't much like. One day in the future, I think the world might need protecting from Crunch Hut. It makes me sad to say it.' She sighed.

Ant began to ask whether they'd argued about Operation Wipeout, but she talked over him. He remembered that she couldn't hear him. Kelly had filmed this many years before.

'So this is where you come in,' she said. 'You and your dragon can now defend any game. I've been training you both up, hoping you will help protect the world from whatever my darling brother has in mind. I'll be watching, too, if I'm still around. So, all I can say is good luck.'

'No, no, no, don't go!' cried Ant, but it was too late: Kelly Crunch sighed, reached over and pressed a button. The video stopped and the screen shrank then disappeared from the sky.

Now it made sense why Kody hated *Kismet* so much: it had been Kelly's creation, not his. Ant started to feel annoyed with Kelly. Why wasn't she here right now, protecting the world from her brother? Where was she?

Ant felt lonelier than ever. Then he remembered he had Griff and Rubie by his side. And, of course, Pradahl. If she were able to play with them in any game, think what that would mean for their games detective agency!

He turned and rubbed her nose and she butted her forehead against his shoulder, then they started to walk through the mist. Before long they came to a curved edge, over which the clouds tumbled like a waterfall. Ant gasped as he saw, a long way below, a slowly rotating disc of stars and planets and masses of cosmic dust.

'It's the whole of Kismet Cosmos,' he whispered, overwhelmed by its beauty. From where they stood, he could pick out the individual planets they both knew so well: Zoberne and Aneome, even tiny Mantros. Now he realised that all those planets had simply been training them up, him and Pradahl, getting them ready for bigger adventures ahead. Kismet Heaven wasn't the end: it was just the beginning.

'Pradahl, our little team has a huge job to do!' said Ant. 'Kody Crunch is bound to try Operation Wipeout again. But between us all, we can take him on.'

Pradahl nudged Ant's shoulder and huffed happy puffs of smoke.